SLOTH

SLOTH

Joanne Askew

Queer Space
New Orleans

Published in the United States of America and United Kingdom by
Queer Space
A Rebel Satori Imprint
www.rebelsatoripress.com

Paperback ISBN: 978-1-60864-180-2
Ebook ISBN: 978-1-60864-181-9
Library of Congress Control Number: 2021947991

"Someone has to stand still for you to love them."
—*Carrie Fisher*

S

An arm reached from the black murky leaf litter. It stretched out its fingers but lost the fight against its own weight and splashed back down to the dark surface. Soon, I saw the head. Its mouth was the only thing above the bog. Eyes, ears, nose, all below the surface, with a gasping mouth at the pinnacle of the mass. You could hear the rasping breaths it tried to take, the way the water had pooled in its mouth, causing bubbles to form as it exhaled. This was Sloth.

"Natali," Lana said. She only said my full first name when something was wrong, or I had stacked the dishwasher incorrectly – I knew it wasn't the latter.

We were in a glade, trees sheltering us. There were a few bodies littered around, mostly over ten months old, barely recognisable as people but for the way their clothes still hung on their skeletons. The fresher ones bore more promise. I checked their wrists, no fitness watches, no watches at all. Someone had been here before us.

It was late winter now, all the skies brought us were rains. It made the ground harder to navigate. Our toes were prunes in our worn-out shoes, our teeth chattered almost constantly with the damp and chill that sunk to our bones. Frost took over the night as mud consumed the day. We never seemed to get dry, to get warm. I looked out across the glade, sheltered by bare trees.

The ground, a seeping blackness, sticky, consuming, hungry to envelop all who neared.

"Should we do something?" I asked Lana.

"You do it. I can't face it." Lana jogged on the spot, lips tight, her eyes wandering to the sky, the trees, but never to me. The squelch of the ground underneath her feet stung my ears.

"Give me the knife." I reached out. She handed it to me, her fist clenched around the hilt. Her grip lingered.

The bog was knee-deep. Deep enough for a small person to almost fully submerge. I was over the goal line within a few seconds, heart rate a hundred-and-three. Each step I took threatened to take my footwear with it, but my laces held true despite the cool trickle of water invading seams. Shoes had become gold to us, fitness watches were diamonds. My boots refilled with stagnant liquid – I would need to dry them off once we found refuge for the night.

The gaping mouth slowly closed, then reopened baring a little pinkness of a tongue. I urged myself forward, through the swampy ground, each step releasing stenches trapped beneath the bog. My shins took most of the effort. They burned with fatigue, but it warmed me, pressed me on. The sky seemed to grey with every breath I took. Condensation hung in the air, obstructed my vision then dissipated into the breeze. Twilight approached.

"Hello?" I called to the mouth. It didn't answer. It probably couldn't find the energy. "It's ok. Everything is ok. It'll be over soon. I'm here to help you." My voice shook. I needed to be strong, share my confidence with the suffering. "I'm nearly there." I was firmer, more reassuring.

My foot stopped near the mouth. Debris pooled around my foot sucking it away from the tiny figure. Their face was revealed, although littered with debris and black tar-like water. It was a

2

girl, maybe six or seven. My heart rate increased way above the goal line. I looked back to Lana. Her lip quivered, maybe in fear, maybe in guilt, maybe she was just cold. She became a mouse, scared of the world rotating beneath her. I became a statue, scared of words leaving my mouth, the wrong words, words that would hurt my wife.

I wouldn't tell her it was a kid. I wanted to let the little girl be free, without pain, let her rest and sink into the mud forever like the virus wanted her to, without another person weeping for her.

I bent down into a squat. My behind dipped into the murk, heels shifting, squelching against my boots. I lifted the girl's head free from the bog, cleared her eyes of debris and let her look at my face. Her eyes flickered.

"It'll be over soon," I whispered, almost cooed.

She blinked, slow like a baby's first steps, incremental movements.

I pulled the knife from my back pocket, careful she didn't see it. It was a military knife, handed out to folks when the British Armed Forces arrived and quickly died like most of us. We had wrapped the handle in cloth so it was easier to grip in the wet weather.

I moved my hand where it cupped her head and supported her neck. The murky water wound through my fingers with strands of her hair. Her head rolled back. I breathed, trying to slow the pounding my pulse caused in my head. Then, gripping until my knuckles were white, I plunged the knife into the child's skull.

"You can sleep now," I said. Her long death had become short. She didn't blink again.

I watched as she sank slowly into the mud. I couldn't tell what colour her hair used to be, what race she was, how thin she had inevitably become over the year of the Sloth. It took most of five minutes for her to fully sink. Lana called to me a few times, but I didn't respond. I didn't want to go back to her, let her see the tears staining my face, see the guilt that was so obvious, the pain my expression showed as I killed the child the same way I had killed ours.

I whimpered slightly and Lana called again. Her voice made a new tear topple from my eye, made my heart swell with the love I had once felt non-stop for her. I looked to my watch. Well over the goal line. I would be ok for three hours, safe from the virus's symptoms, symptoms that were irreversible, led to a slow death once they had set in. I could rest a little, take my time. Be the brave one, for Lana.

I built the fire in silence an hour later, words too afraid to come from my lips. My mag stick was running out - the last reminder of how the British government tried to save us, before they realised they still needed to save themselves. From the window of the stable we had found, Lana watched rain fall. It smelled of the kind of must that settled in a cluttered garden shed over the winter. The straw was covered in a black mould, but there was a roof over us, a chance to get warm again.

"Lana, you need to run. Just run for a little, then we can eat."

"I already have." She didn't look to me when she spoke.

"I didn't see you."

"I did." She continued to gaze, drowning in something, a thought, a memory.

"Well, I'm going to set an alarm for two hours." I stood, hoping she would look at me. She didn't. "Lana, where are you? Get out of your head."

She stayed as still as the dead, or like a mouse frozen in fear.

"It's better in there."

"Remember what we said when this all started? We said we'd fight. We said it didn't matter that we couldn't afford the drugs. We said we'd fight like we fought to be together, to have Cain."

"I know."

"Then why does it feel like you've given up?"

"It's been a year since it all went to shit. I thought we would have been saved by now. Instead, we're all dead, everyone, or displaced like us. We see more bodies every day, and less people. We haven't seen anyone in a week, Tali. We're running from ourselves. Maybe the other option would have been better." She shuffled her fitness watch and took off into the grey night. She ran across the overgrown field that held the stable and slowed to a jog around its perimeters. She did twenty loops of the field, then sat at its furthest edge until I could no longer see her outline in the night. I think she was weeping. The wind carried sobs to me, but they could have been an echo in my own mind.

I ran when my alarm went off with a dull hum, and Lana came back to the stable. When I was done, I found her curled by the fire on a bed of rotting straw. Her eyes were closed, but I wasn't sure if she was sleeping. I thought about setting an alarm for her, to make sure she ran, got to the goal line so Sloth wouldn't set in, but doing that would show her I had no faith in her, that I thought she couldn't take care of herself.

Cain's death, his succumbing to Sloth, was fast compared to what I witnessed every day with her. The darkness pooling in her eyes hurt me as much as it hurt her. The inevitability of her moods, the snapping of her voice, the way there was nothing I could do to help her plagued me. My words, when they came, were wrong. My gestures didn't move her. I felt like Sloth had already set into me, like we talked less and less each day because there was nothing more to say in a country rotting around us. I was weak, impotent to the black beast of depression, despite how hard I tried to bring Lana back from the dead.

At eight PM, my alarm went off and I ran. At eleven, I did it again, tears cooling on my face like an icy touch as I ran against the wind. At two AM, I woke Lana to see if she had run. She told me she had. We were always out of sync at night. We ran whilst the other slept and vice versa. During a bout of sleep, I dreamt Lana left me, wandering off into the broken world on her own. I screamed for her, searched for her, but only found the ghost of the Lana I loved before Sloth, a version of her full of light, full of wit, and joy. I screamed to that Lana, but she faded into mist. When my alarm went off for me to run, I was already above the goal line.

In the morning, she hummed a song as she pulled on her dry boots. Baby, It's Cold Outside. I have always hated that song, and I knew she did, too. It didn't stop her humming the melody, singing the occasional word. I joined in after a while, quietly, because I didn't want to stop her singing. She had the most beautiful voice. She never knew. It came out of her like a secret, needing to be lured, almost tempted out by a gentle beat or a hum.

The first time I heard her sing was the morning after we made love for the first time. She was making coffee, back when we had coffee. She was smiling, humming as the morning light hit her face. Back then, she had short brunette hair that gently stroked her shoulders as she moved, big brown eyes that glistened with optimism. She took compliments back then, almost snatched them from me and revelled in the love we had, the love I showed her through my words. Her humming turned into lyrics, some Dire Straits hit from long ago. I'm pretending I don't know exactly what song it was, but I do, I remember every lyric she uttered, every note that hung in the air with the beams of sunlight. You and me, Babe, how 'bout it?

She sang to Cain, too. I used to crouch behind the door of his nursery as she guided him into a peaceful sleep with her voice. When he was a little older, he started to sing too, but he wasn't as shy as Lana. His untamed vocals echoed around our flat back in London, mostly formed of made up words, gurgles and giggles. A lump formed in my throat. Something so wonderful, so wanted, caused a gut-wrenching pang in my heart. They say you should remember the dead, but it was too painful. That pain was more apparent in Lana, and every day since Cain died, I wished I could crawl inside her heart and take it all away.

The sun rose on our ugly reality and graced her messy long hair with a lick of honey. Streaks of light crossed her neck, ran across her breasts where they lay wrapped in a beige woollen jumper far too big for her. I think it used to be clean and white, but nothing was that pure anymore.

"Shall we head north?" she asked without looking at me.

I rose from the rotting straw that had been my bed. "Ready for the Spring?"

She turned but didn't look at me. "Yes. Cain loved it when the daffodils bloomed." She wrapped her arms around herself. "We can reach Fort William in a few weeks. They say there's a benefactor there taking advantage of how the altitude makes our hearts beat faster. Some Scottish community that takes care of people. They don't have the drugs, but they have exercise equipment, food, warmth. They even have alarms to remind everyone to run." Her voice throbbed with the morning's gentle light. It seemed godly to me, she always had, like a secret lioness who let out her roars when you least expected it. I wish I could have told her just how celestial she was to me.

"Lana, we don't know if that's true." She was referring to a traveller we had met a few weeks ago. The man was heading to Fort William. Said he had worked for a company before Sloth, and the company was helping people now with the resources they had in the mountains. He cursed the government and their buffoon of a leader, who, instead of helping his nation, locked himself in his own ivory tower and encouraged his wealthy peers to do the same, some with their penthouses, some with their country estates. The man on the road said he had been one of them, but their selfishness had worried him and he took to the roads to be a refugee rather than be like them. He said some of them had some twisted ideas, but he didn't elaborate; it shook his voice too much.

"What do we do then, Tali? Do we just keep running? We already lost what we love the most," Lana said, mouse-like.

"No, Lana. We still have each other." I screwed my face at her, a waiting look to see if I had said the wrong thing.

"I know. We need to have a goal besides a hundred and three. Let this be our goal. Let Fort William be our home. Even if we don't find that place, we'll have still have spring, but in the mountains." She smiled the same way she smiled at Cain when she wanted him to eat his veggies.

She seemed like she had been mulling this over for some time. I had been too, every day since we had met that man. But his accent made me uncomfortable. He reminded me of the bankers in the city, the ones who never offered their seat for pregnant women, or walked around constantly on their phones talking about board meetings or deadlines, or growth hacking, brand guidelines and other CEO buzzwords.

But there was also hope in his eyes, the kind of hope I longed to see since the country went to shit. All human eyes had become dull. No shine graced irises. No lips curled into smiles. Laughs were as dead as most of the UK. This man was different; he had turned from a wanderer to a man on a path with a destination. A destination, I thought. It would fill me with purpose, a direction.

"Okay. We'll go north," I said, my lips going from a frown to something more neutral.

Lana smiled. Her smiles over the past year had been as elusive as a warm meal. The version of her in my mind faltered. A shadow covered her face like a large bird blocking out the sun, brief, colossal, consuming but inevitable. My shoulders tensed. She was as unpredictable as the new world we lived it. I swallowed. Bravery reared inside my cracked heart.

"You're so beautiful, you know that, Lana?" I gazed at her. She was my goddess, my Gaia, my lioness. You appreciate your wife so much more when the world is full of the hate that wanted to keep us apart. And now, even more so, since the world became full of death, disease, the putrid blackness wanting everyone to die.

She didn't reply. She smiled again and I revelled in that moment of sweetness, for it might be some time till I had it again.

L

We ran, on and off, for several miles north through Coventry, guided only by a cheap Christmas cracker compass. The main roads were gauntlets of abandoned cars, litter blowing in the wind. The smaller roads were hard to navigate, the vegetation taking over, covering signs, covering the sky. We kept our eyes peeled for a map, but the world had moved on from physical maps some years ago and hadn't expected a collapse like this. We searched older looking cars, those with blue badges, hoping the older generation still held on to paper information. We hadn't found one yet.

Sometimes, the mud was so thick, we didn't need to run to hit the goal line. Our hearts worked harder to pull our feet from the swampy land. Sometimes, the fear of approaching strangers made our hearts race. Sometimes the tears that snuck down Lana's face made mine reach the goal line, my heart reaching out, wanting to help her, not being able to as she shook, rocked with the grief.

"Lana, baby." I took her hand as she jogged ahead of me, ready to take a different gauntlet, a gauntlet of words. "We need to talk."

She turned, with a sickly smile I knew was fake. My heart raced, anticipating a fight. I wanted to talk to her, really talk, get some kind of window into her unpredictability.

She sat back on the bonnet of a Ford Mondeo that used to be blue, but now wore a robe of greyish dirt. The road was littered with dust, weeds, patches of mud. Only a few abandoned cars scattered the middle lanes, most lay upturned or in ditches near the hard shoulder where their drivers had not reached their goal lines, despite the anxiety that must have been flooding through their veins, and had slowed down behind the wheel. In the gaps there weren't cars, there were bodies. The smell greeted you like a friend you were avoiding. Once the scent took hold of your nose, it never seemed to leave. It was the fragrance of England now. Picked clean by crows and animals, beige bones flew flags of rotting material, stripes, spots, some seventies metal band T-shirts that had been all the rage just before Sloth. A raven stood atop a rib cage wrapped in an ACDC shirt; like a twisted album cover inviting you into the madness.

We were on the A68 just north of Durham, planning to make it to Edinburgh in hopes there would be a sign to Loch Lomond. From there, we could head north west to Loch Linnhe and follow it inland to Fort William. We didn't want to set another goal for ourselves to get there, our only goal, the goal line, was too important to stick too.

"Tali, what?" Lana asked.

My nostrils flared, heart pounding against my chest. Words were not my enemy, the wrong ones were. I retreated. I was not brave enough right now to challenge her. What would I even say? What could I even say?

"You remember when we rode those red bikes through London on Chinese New Year?" I deescalated, hoping she wouldn't notice the sudden come down from the build-up.

"Yeah? What about it?" she snapped.

We laughed so hard on those red bikes, under the red lanterns that graced the rooftops of China Town. She stopped regularly to talk to vendors, waved madly at tourists, especially children with eyes full of golden wonder. She gave crisp twenty-pound notes to the homeless of London, even when she had to go to a cash point to get it. That's the night I learned she had a heart full of acceptance and love, but not full enough to ever stop it growing further. I was trying to reminisce with her, make her remember the fun we had before the country faded away, make her remember the woman I fell for, because honestly? I thought that might have been the right tact.

"We should look for bikes, that's all. We'll get there quicker then." She knew that wasn't where I was originally going. I pawed at my nose ring. It rested uncomfortably at its seam.

"Just take it out," she snapped. "Just take the goddam thing out. It doesn't matter anymore." She finally looked at me, really looked at me.

"It matters to me. It matters to who I am, my identity. Lana, we can't forget who we are." My voice cracked at the end. "They've won if we forget who we are."

"They've already won, Tali. We're animals now."

"Then we keep fighting, okay, like animals." I lifted her chin, my own mouth craving her touch. My skin contrasted against hers, olive and milky ivory. "If we kneel and let the virus take us, let the one per cent frolic and drink and be merry, protected from the real world, then we are no better than animals to them. You get it?"

Lana's eyes glazed slightly. There was a rim of tears dangerously close to the edge as I looked into them. She wouldn't let them fall, I knew her too well. She turned her head away from me, but I followed her eye line, moved around so she couldn't avoid me and sink lower into the blackness that threatened to take her every day.

"Babe, we're fighters, yeah?"

She sniffed and nodded. Her face, once soft and glowing, now was gaunt, her pale skin barely covering her cheek bones.

"Things are shit. Other countries thrive while we stay here in this wasteland, no one to help us, no foreign aid. But that's ok. You said it was better that way."

She pulled her jumper over her hands like a child. "Because we can't risk it getting out, destroying the world. One-way ticket. The land of the lost," she said without looking up.

When the first cases arose on the Isle of Man, they closed off the ferries to the mainland. Those cases struck a retirement home first, not much risk of it getting out. But when it spread to a panicked island nation, confined to their tiny rock, unable to leave, the entire of the UK closed its borders, knowing due to past failures, how easy it would be to infect the world. They say it was a wealthy Manx businessman that took to his private helicopter and came to the mainland, a wealthy Manx businessman that doomed the entire nation to quarantine.

"We are a rock. We are an island," I sang to Lana, completely off-key.

A smile broke on her face. "Remember the rice?"

"Surprise rice." I sat by her side, my hand on her knee. The car creaked under both our weight.

"I'd give anything for a bowl of rice stuffed with sauce right now."

"We can scavenge for something similar. Maybe tinned stew. I'll make you that rice. It's our anniversary in a week. We can celebrate." I widened my eyes, let my lips curl into a cute smile, the kind that made her lean in for a kiss.

She sniffed again and folded her arms across her chest. Her

face was skeletal. Bags graced her beautiful eyes. "Maybe," was all she said.

My heart dropped. It felt like unrequited love, like rejection at high school. I stood from the Mondeo bonnet and kicked at the ground, heard her shuffle too. I knew she was suffering, her heart filling with black like our footsteps through the bog, but I needed her, needed to feel loved by her, even if it was just a smile.

When I turned back round to her, she was on all-fours, wiping the dust from the car's windscreen. I was taken aback, but I couldn't keep my eyes off her behind.

"Look!" she cried. "A map!" She turned, distracting me from her ass. A light appeared in her eyes for the inanimate object. She hopped down from the bonnet, tried the passenger side door; it was open. She grinned at me when it sprung as freely as we used to feel, clambered inside and snatched it like a pirate grasping for a bounty. Her joy was infectious; it always had been, no matter how rare it had become.

I thought of Cain. Thought of the moments I watched him and Lana from across rooms, across halls, car seats. How they laughed and smiled and looked each other right in the eye like they had a secret language. I wanted to tell her, tell her how I admired her as a mother, as a partner. But I couldn't remind her of our loss, of the space Cain left behind. Remembering him brought her more pain than the collapse of the UK ever could.

We heard footsteps, the kind that echoed against tarmac and shook silent air. We both looked up at the same time. Lana's smile broke, my thoughts of her and Cain evaporated. Three men jogged towards us, huge bags on their backs, much bigger than our own backpacks. They slowed as they saw us, checked their fitness watches. One just rested his fingers on his wrist. Their mouths sported uneasy smiles.

I turned to Lana. Her face was stone. I smiled, placed my hand on her knee and turned back to the men, with an aching grin forced out of me like the last drop of toothpaste.

I turned to her, made it seem like I was brushing a stray hair behind my ear. "Be ready to run," I whispered.

"Ladies," one said. He was slight, had a scruffy black beard only a few tones darker than his skin, couldn't have been any older than twenty-five. His clothes were old gym clothes, active-wear with holes in the knees and elbows. The other two men held back, flanking him like silent partners.

I nodded in response, threw my bag on my back. Sometimes, we had to hide that we were married. We lied and said we were friends. Some people still didn't agree with our love, we learned that the hard way.

A drop of rain fell on my cheek. The man felt it too. He reached his hands out as if to catch the sparse water. A twitch formed on my lips. My body was urging me to run, preparing me to take Lana's hand and flee for our lives. I imagined the cloth grip of the knife, how I'd reach for it as we bolted away, just in case they caught up with us, subjected us to whatever torment they were thinking, robbing us, killing us, raping us.

"Do you trade?" their apparent leader asked, coming to a stop by the Mondeo. He rested his hand on the car.

Lana's eyes darted to him with disgust.

My lips twitched again. My palms grew hot, throbbing with a new layer of sweat.

"No," I said. "We don't have much to trade." My voice didn't tremble. It was hard and sure, too sure, maybe aggressive.

"We were looking for a map, mate. Checked all the petrol stations – wiped out. See you got one." He pointed to Lana, his London accent a comfort to my ears, despite the possible menace his actions held.

Her lips were tight, drawn out across her face.

I felt my body try to lurch towards her, to protect her.

"It took us a while to find it. It's not up for trade." I edged in front of her, let my eyes glance down the double-laned road that would have hummed in rush hour, looking for the right direction to run.

"I'll teach you how to measure your heart rate without one of those watches, and…" The man looked around as I had, a breeze caught his beard. "I got a bar of chocolate," he said, his eyes returning to us.

"You think because we're women we're looking for fucking chocolate?" Lana snapped, a hiss remaining on her lips after her words. When society was intact, that comment would have made me laugh, but now, every decision, every choice, affected whether you lived or died.

The man held up his hands. "No, mate, not like that."

"You a doctor?" I interrupted before Lana could say anymore.

"No, mate. I was a nurse. The name's Mohamed. I picked these two up about six months ago in a car wreck. Daniel and Ryan. We won't hurt you."

I surveyed the group with suspicious eyes, watched the way their legs idly twitched, their palms rested against their legs, their backpack straps. Mohamed's cheeks were raised, like a gesture of friendliness without the full smile.

"Tali. This is my friend, Lana," I said, after a pause.

Lana rolled her eyes. "Wife. I'm her wife," she spat.

"Lana," I warned without looking back to her.

I heard her slide off the Mondeo, brush herself down. She stood by me, close enough I could feel her clothes sway as she moved.

"You wanna share a meal?" Mohamed asked. "We don't need to move for another three."

I felt Lana pull at my sleeve, urging me to say no.

"We won't hurt you. That's not our jam," Mohamed said.

There was silence.

Lana didn't take her eyes off them. I let mine wander, allowed them space whilst I considered the danger. A telegraph pole stuck into the air at an odd angle where it had been hit by a car, it made all the lines loose, linking together more like drooping Christmas lights than electric wires. All three of them looked to where I was gazing.

"You gotta make up your mind. It's gonna get dark. The main roads ain't safe."

"What do you mean, not safe?" Lana snapped.

"Mate. You ain't travelled much on the motorways or A roads?"

"Not much. We just wandered for the year, keeping to the countryside," I replied.

"Well, then trade me your map, for a lesson in pulse taking, and also some wise words. I don't wanna ever see you on these roads after dark."

"We'll do what we want," Lana said. Her big eyes narrowed.

"These roads used to be well travelled. That was the problem. Too many of us in one spot. Too easy for them."

"Who?" Lana asked, stepping forward.

"Let's get off the road. I'll tell you over a warm fire."

"Fine, but I'm having the chocolate," Lana said.

I looked at Lana. She wasn't joking.

✖

I built the fire. It was something I was good at. The men watched in awe, offering me their lighters. I refused. No point in wasting lighter fluid when a simple spark could create what we needed. I struck at my mag stick only twice before a bright spark settled within the dry tinder and turned quickly into an orange blaze.

The crackle of the fire echoed around the bridge we had settled under. It lit graffiti on the wall. Clown faces, lions, elephants littered the concrete. A looming sloth in a plague mask overcast them all. One phrase shone in red against the pictures: "You thought Brexit was bad?"

Lana kept the map inside her jumper, like they would snatch it at any point.

"You had any close calls?" Mohamed asked.

"With Sloth? Or with guys like you?"

"Lana," I scolded.

Mohamed smiled. "You ain't got to worry about us, mate. Same team. It's the one percent you've got to worry about."

"No different to before Sloth then," I said.

Mohamed smiled. "Yeah, when the NHS collapsed, the exec board left their posts just before they announced the closure of the service. Like they were getting out of the blast zone, protecting themselves."

"Doesn't surprise me," I said. "No doubt they took the meds they needed to keep Sloth at bay."

"Yep, the shelves were clean, mate, every type of cardiostimulatory drug you could think of. Have you seen any of them now?" he said.

18

"No, they wouldn't dare leave their safehouses."

Mohamed's eyes grew wide. His dark irises grew, pupils dilating to tiny black specks over the firelight. He leaned forward. "That's where you're wrong, mate. They started coming out when things got real quiet. At first, under guard, I think they were just curious. But someone, some twisted fuck, started the Safari." Mohamed quieted.

"The Safari?"

"It's exactly how sounds," the pale one, Daniel, chirped in, a Polish accent gracing his words, almost like my father's Ukrainian tone. He held up a hand. "Now, we not saying they're all bad. We've met a few gooduns, but this troop, like maybe three or four truck's worth, clearly had taste for blood."

"They come in armoured vehicles, a gunman on the front, hunting the most dangerous game – people." Mohamed leaned in, the fire flickering on his dark skin. "They have a points system, we're sure."

"We heard one of them shout 'single' when they took down Sarah. She was slowing. Sloth had taken her. She missed raising her heart rate by about five minutes. They killed her sister too. Shouted 'five.'"

"Daniel, mate, easy on the details," Mohamed said, twisting his fingers through his beard.

"Sarah was worth one point to them, Mo." Daniel's face creased. "Skurwysyn. Sons of bitches," he muttered, slipping into his native tongue. The third man, Ryan, poked at the fire, silent as the country itself.

"They come at night. Honking, hollering. Looking for runners. At the start, they never left the armoured trucks, now, they're levelling up in a way, innit?" He looked to his comrades, they nodded.

Lana leaned in. "What do you mean 'levelling up'?"

"I mean, they're making their game harder now. Taking to hunting us on foot."

"So, we're worth five points to them?" she asked.

"Yes, you are. Men are worth six. Elderly, three. Kids… ten." Mohamed gulped.

"How do you even know that?" I prompted him. "Seems dangerous for them, to want to come down to ground zero."

"We make it our mission to talk to anyone we meet on the road. Exchange information. At first for anything that might cure us, a research lab or safe house, but the danger isn't Sloth anymore. It's what we've heard at nights, what we've run from." Mohamed looked to Ryan. Ryan was pale, thinner than the others, hadn't spoken yet, but never took his eyes off the conversation.

"First time they found us, we were sleeping in a lorry on the hard shoulder of the M25," Mohamed continued. "There was a bigger group of us then. We had six. Jhanvi got up to run. She was only going to do a dash up to Junction Eleven and back, but she never came back. I woke the rest of our group up and we went out into the night looking for her. As soon as we found her with a bullet hole in her neck, beams of light blinded us." He sniffed.

"These trucks were beltin' down the motorway, innit." His hand shook against his knee in a perfect pattern, a beat almost. "They had snow ploughs on the front, a mounted Gatling on the back, a driver dressed in black, and a few well-dressed white men in the back, armed. When I say 'well-dressed', I mean they were suited and booted, tuxes and bowties. They had megaphones too, were calling out, trying to coax others out from hiding. Nothing convincing about a man in a suit saying he'll save us all, innit. We scattered, ran for the cover of trees by the road. We didn't have our bags, our supplies."

Daniel sharply inhaled, wiping a tear from his eye. "Lost all our loot. Lost our Jhanvi."

Mohamed placed a palm on Daniel's shoulder. "We started again from scratch. Came back the next day to bury her but her body was gone."

Daniel's eyes swam with tears. "We argued so much that week. Couldn't understand why those men did it. We actually thought they were like us at first, just refugees who had turned violent with no police to control them. Then we met this family from the city. They told us they hunkered down in Canary Wharf for the first few months, until they started seein' these massive fucking trucks coming out of fancy apartment block carparks, the kind of apartment block that had a penthouse. Took us a few more weeks of talking to others to work it all out. Looks like some of the one percent got a little stir-crazy inside, made a new sport," Daniel said, his accent thicker with his emotion. "A blood sport."

"That's fucking crazy," Lana said. "Can't be true."

"You've been off the main roads this whole time. Trust me, fam. It's true." Mohamed poked at the fire. "From what we've pieced together, they're a group of twenty or so."

There was a silence, just for a few minutes. Then, like a perfectly timed punchline, a car horn sounded somewhere in the distance, tires screeched, gun shots finished the cacophony of noise. They echoed in the outdoor silence like a symbol on a grave.

Lana and I flattened our bodies against the ground. Sparks and embers jumped into the air as Mohamed stamped out the fire. Ryan pulled out a baseball bat, wrapped his hands around it like a fresh sandwich just passed over a counter to him. Daniel darted against the bridge wall pulling Ryan with him by his coat hood.

21

"Wall," Daniel barked under his breath.

I crawled, dragging Lana with me, and pulled our bodies up against the bridge wall. Mohamed joined us after covering the entire fire with his coat. It didn't catch, but it steamed as the damp evaporated into the air.

The noises grew. Stopping every few seconds but returning with increased volume. I spotted a torch still on by Lana's backpack. I went to crawl to it, extinguish the symbol of our location, but Mohamed's arm forced me back.

He crawled, reached for the torchlight and turned it off. The click echoed from the bricks above. He didn't return to us; he didn't have time.

The yelp of tires made the bridge above us quiver. Shouts soon followed. Then a series of slaps against tarmac, footsteps.

A well-spoken voice called out. "Can you smell that? Fire. I can smell a fire."

My eyes caught Mohamed's. He raised a single finger to his lips in a hush.

I looked to Lana. Her eyes were wide, her mouth open so she could steady her breaths. She slowly looked upwards to where the commotion was coming from. There was a gunshot. She flinched and didn't reopen her eyes.

My fingers found her in the darkness. She was digging her nails into the ground. I eased them free, let her wrap them around mine, tight.

"Boss, I saw a fire on the way up. By the roadside. Abandoned."

There was a shuffle, the sound of spitting. "Should have fucking told me back there then."

"Boss, there were no people around it."

"But it's a start point for a hunt, you twat."

Lana's eyes were still closed as car doors slammed, a motor accelerated against a cluttered road. When the engine was far enough away, Mohamed rose and brushed himself off. He pulled his coat from the fire. It was warped, burned stuffing melted to a grey tangle of melted plastic.

"Like that," he finally said.

"Who are they?" Lana was sobbing. She rose, wiping tears from her chin.

"Some people aren't good people. No matter what the state of the world is. There will always be terrible people."

"What now then? For you?" I asked him.

He shrugged. As his shoulders came down, he let out a smile. "This, I guess. First it was all about survival, then for a while we thought about getting a permanent home. But now, I guess we got our calling, innit. We're just travelling round, letting others know about the Safari."

"Like missionaries."

"Somefin' like that." He exhaled like he hadn't taken a breath for a while.

"We were planning to take the main roads to Scotland," I said, more of a question to him. Lana nudged me as I spoke.

"I'd rethink that," Mohamed said. "The motorways are their network of hunting grounds."

"Are you okay, Ryan?" Lana singled him out.

He was still on the ground, rocking himself, knees pressed to his face.

"He's deaf. He's teaching me to sign, so I can communicate with him," Mohamed jumped in. "Shakes him up because he can't hear them coming."

"I can sign." I knelt in front of Ryan.

I rested my hands on him, waking him from panic. I spelled

out my name on my fingers. He responded with a smile.

"My father was deaf," I said out loud and signing to Ryan. "He said it was punishment for producing a gay daughter."

Ryan rolled his eyes, shook a finger, brought his hands together and pushed them in at the connection between the thumb and index finger, what the fuck? His eyes were red, bloodshot.

I laughed, hoping to reassure him. "Christians." I signed it's okay though, but didn't say it out loud. That was only for me and Ryan. "He lost his hearing in a construction accident when I was twelve. When I came out at twenty, he said 'Now I get it, God is punishing me for the abomination I raised.'"

"Where is he now?" Ryan signed.

"The Safari man? Or my father?" I signed.

"Father."

"Dead. Sloth killed the elderly first." I always hated signing 'dead'. It seemed to linger in my hands.

"Most of them," Mohamed said. He was scrapping the burned parts from his coat. "So, why Scotland?"

Lana's hand found my thigh like she was telling me to be quiet. I obeyed. "Mountain air," I settled on.

"Nothing to do with this sanctuary everyone is talking about?"

"Mo, when you call it a 'sanctuary', it usually ends up being some kind of twisted cult," Daniel said. I continued to translate the conversation to Ryan.

"Fine, facility. You heard about it?"

"Yeah. We might check it out."

"Might," Lana interrupted.

"We'll end up there eventually, but for now, you've shown us we have more work to do on the roads, spreading the word about the Safari," Mohamed said.

"We just want to stay alive," Lana said.

"Let me show you how to count your pulse then." Mohamed reached out a hand to Lana. She took it. "This will be more accurate than those watches, keep you going for a lot longer too."

"Fine." Lana smiled, looked sideways at me like she was admitting defeat, that these men were kind and helpful.

It was in those moments I saw flashes of her old self. She was irate, high maintenance, neurotic, but she knew it. It was true beauty to recognise your flaws, even more so to take the piss out of yourself. Lana did that. She could get away with murder, all because she owned it.

The first time we met, I was a barista. She ordered a cappuccino; told me she didn't want the chocolate sprinkles. She came back into the coffee shop five minutes later complaining that she wanted the sprinkles. When I explained to her, I had asked and she had said no, she gave in, flustered with smiles. Said she was too busy checking emails and hadn't heard me properly. I called her a 'bitch' under my breath as she turned to leave. She heard. She stopped, turned with the brightest smile I had ever seen, said, "Thank you," and wished me a good day.

She came back the next day, and the day after that. On her third return, she took me home. It wasn't attraction at first, it was the feeling of being challenged by someone, an equal. It was like she was goading me, daring me to fall for her. I did. More than I ever knew I could. I rubbed my finger and thumb together, something I did when I thought of Lana, thought of how soft her hair had been to my hands that morning we first woke up together.

"Tali, come see." Lana grabbed my wrist, fidgeting her fingers to find my pulse. "Mo, show Tali now," she ordered. She passed my hand over to him, and stood, jogging on the spot.

Mohamed looked at Lana and smiled.

"Yeah," I said. "Sorry about her."

"I like her," he said adjusting my fingers to find my own pulse.

"She keeps you on your toes, for sure." I altered my fingers, guided by his. I could feel it. A gentle throb from a world beneath my skin. "Got it."

"Good, now use this." He passed me a smashed-up wristwatch. "Count your beats for fifteen seconds on this watch, then multiply your beats by four. That's your heart rate. If you get good, like me, you won't need the wristwatch. When you're out there, look for a stopwatch. It'll be easier then. Check gyms, pools, schools. We had a few, but we gave them all out to others."

"You guys really are the good guys, huh?" I said. I thought of the NHS staff who tried to stick it out, tried to find out about the rules of the virus, tried to emulate antibodies to ward it off like the last close call. They stayed in the hospitals long after they had closed down, long after all funding and deliveries were stripped from them. They tried to carry on their work when the UK's infrastructure collapsed. It didn't work, it just couldn't.

"Just remember, Tali. Remember what this country was like, who made it special. It wasn't those right-wingers in their Armani. It was us, people like us, the salt of the earth." Mohamed's frown hardened. His lightness, his easy way, dissolved. "We should get away now, make some distance between them and us. Do you believe me now?"

"Yes. We'll stay off the main roads. Practise the pulse taking. Take the map we found. You missionaries will make better use of it."

"Thank you. Tali, stay off those roads. I'm serious, mate." His lips stayed parted.

"We got it, Mohamed. We've lost someone too. We're careful,

especially around others. Sloth isn't the only thing we're scared of." I looked to Lana, still checking her pulse.

"Hundred and three." She mock punched the air having recovered from her fright. I worried that her depression was an infinite fall, worried the black dog would be too much for her, worried that I wasn't enough for her after we lost Cain. Her strength was understated, slow to rise, quick to make an impact.

Mohamed, Daniel and Ryan left after we handed over the map. Lana took their chocolate and buried it in her pack. We headed north through the night, turning the other way when we reached bigger roads. We were both jumpy, scared of the voices that sought people, scared of missing our goal lines by even a few minutes.

In my mind, Lana was a mouse cowering in a corner. The shadow of a cat approached, growing larger and larger as it neared. She trembled. Silent tears polluted her face, as our fear polluted my image of her.

O

We found horses the next day. They were malnourished, in a field nearly brown with mud. Ivy and brambles, growing over the barbed wires fences, kept them in. There were three. One bay, two chestnuts, around fourteen hands each. They weren't big horses, but they'd carry our weight with ease. A body lay peacefully on the other side of the fence, curled up like it only wanted to take a nap. Its smell had soaked into the surrounding area, polluting it with death.

"Should we set them free?" Lana asked, pulling her backpack up on her shoulders.

"We could ride them. There's a tack room."

She screwed up her face. I had said the wrong thing again. Lana grew up in the city. Myself, I was born in the home counties, close to London, but further enough away that I was used to livestock. I had ridden horses as a young girl. I was the only working-class kid in riding class. All the pretty blonde Surrey girls who went to private schools like Charterhouse and Eton never spoke to me. I don't blame them, I blame their parents for never allowing them a wider view on the world, society. I wasn't an expert horseman by any means, but I knew how to saddle one, tighten the girth and get a bit in a strong and dangerous mouth.

"I can show you, Lana, if you trust me."

"I trust you. I just don't trust them." She edged further from the paddock, as if her body language would portray her truth rather than her words.

"I think we should. Those fucking men last night, Lana. They made my stomach lurch. I haven't been that scared, not since Cain. I think we could get further away from them too, still raise our pulses on a canter every three hours," I pushed, knowing I was putting my heart in danger challenging her.

"What's a canter?" She wrinkled her nose.

"Like a slow gallop."

"A slow gallop still sounds too fast. What if I fall?"

"I won't let you."

"We have enough to deal with. Let's go." She turned to jog away.

I thought of the mouse she could be, and of the lion she really was. I could be a lion too. "Lana, let's talk about this. I would feel safer on horseback. You would too, after what we heard last night."

She froze, mid step. "I told you I didn't want to." Her words had sharp edges.

"You didn't. You picked holes in my suggestion." In my mind, I was puffing out my chest, making myself seem braver, smarter. In truth I was fiddling at my sleeve soothing my nerves with the texture of my waxed coat.

Lana turned, her body tense. "Not this again." She stepped towards me. Her boots squelched in the mud. "You can't push me to do something I don't want to do."

"And you can't avoid new experiences all your life."

Her mouth dropped open. "I am not. I am keeping us safe."

"No, Lana. I keep us safe. You inject your anxiety into everything we do, even when we're fine." My words were dangerous, harsh, tempting her into combat.

29

"Honey, I am not like you. I am not a free spirit. Being a fucking lesbian does not automatically qualify me to be brave."

"In my experience, I had to be brave."

"Yeah, well I'm sorry your parents were pricks. I'm sorry you're damaged from that. I'm not. And I won't risk anything unless it's necessary."

"Will you try? Just for me?" I softened.

"No. Natali, I won't try horse riding when the whole fucking country is either dead, dying, or trying to kill us now, apparently." She said it like it was final. It wasn't to me.

"Fine. You do what you want. I'm saddling up the bay, see how he copes."

She laughed, took a quick glance at me to see if I was serious, then pulled the sleeves of her jumper to her mouth. Her temple sported a vein.

"If they're dangerous, I'll know it and we can free them and leave them alone."

She looked up at me, the sleeve of the cream jumper masking her lips, covering the expressions she had whilst she was thinking it through. "Fine."

I had to turn away from her. My face suddenly donned a sly smile tempted out of its cave by her. I called to the horses. They looked up at me straight away. One of them took a step towards me, eager, humans a sign of food. Lana settled on a fence behind me, arms crossed like she was ready to tell me she told me so.

I picked up a bucket filled with stagnant water and emptied it. The murky dark liquid pooled around my feet, toppling over grooves in the ground, penetrating clumps of weeds. All three horses watched me. Their ears pricked up. One, the bay, stepped forward. I turned my back on them, walking to the wooden tack room. Over my shoulder, Lana stared at me. The horses had come right up to the fence, their eyes firmly on me.

The tack room door crumbled under my touch. Impregnated with damp, it released its form, splintering to the floor. I stepped over the dank mess. The light from outside filtered in, over saddles hung from the wall, rugs draped over rafters, bridles tangled in heaps. I found the bins lined up against the wall, one labelled 'Alfa A', another with 'molasses'. I took my bucket, filled it with a mix of the two, scrapping off the mould that had constructed a barrier over the horse feed.

When I emerged, the sun had come out from behind clouds that never seemed to disappear. Lana was in the field, with the three horses, touching them on their withers, smiling with child-like glee. I laughed, bit my lip at the sight, at her unpredictability.

Her eyes creeping wider with a sudden focus. "What?" She raised one hand, kept the other on the bay horse. "They're nice, turns out." She turned back to the horse, twiddling its knotted mane with her long pale fingers. "I want this one," she whispered, more to the animal than to me.

"Ten years I've been with you, and shit, girl. You still surprise me."

"I surprise myself too." Her smile leaked into her eyes. "Can I call her Jenny?"

I strode over, ducking to catch sight of underneath the bay. "It's a gelding. A boy."

"Well, he's still called Jenny."

"Try petting him on the flank, work down to his butt. See if he trusts you." She did, smiling as her hands graced his thin body.

"It's working, Tali. I'm a horse lady now." She angled her body away from the beast, arm outstretched so she could still move away if she needed to.

I laughed, put one foot on the lowest rung on the fence and

poured the feed in their empty trough. All three bolted forward, but Lana didn't flinch; she was a horse lady now.

We watched the three creatures tuck into their first real meal in some time. Grass wasn't enough to sustain a working horse in the winter. Two were geldings, one a mare. The chestnut mare seemed a little shy of us. She had a bright white blaze down her face, and socks of white that flared into long feathers.

"We won't ride the mare. She's a little scared still. But she can follow us, maybe she'll learn to trust us."

"What are you gonna call yours? That orange one?"

"Chestnut. Yours is bay. I'll call him Chester, so you learn the proper horse colours."

She laughed, cackled almost. "Fucking Chester and Jenny. What about the mare?"

"Tiger-Lilly. Because she's a flight risk."

Lana looked up from her new pal, Jenny. "I love it. I love you." She stared at me, eye glistening, wet.

I tried not to let my brow furrow, but it did. I guess Lana had those moments too, the moments when I looked at her and realised how lucky I was to have met her, to call her mine. I think she was looking back at me thinking of how we had fallen in love. I hoped she was.

"You're a beautiful horse lady. Now I need to teach you a few things before we move off."

She nodded, took her hand off Jenny, and climbed gracefully over the fence. The horses finished their meal and stood idly in the field, in a daze of contentment.

"Sorry I was a wimp about the ponies."

I glanced up, smiling at her word choice. "I'm just proud of you."

"You are?"

"Yeah, you're a lot braver than you realise." My words came easier when she was happier.

"I'm really not, Tali."

We jogged on the spot for ten minutes and checked our pulses. Then, we pulled out the tangle of bridles into the day light and began to sort through them. They were labelled. One for Sparkles, another for Chad, and a final one for Cinnamon. We laughed at the names.

"I can't ride a Chad. I have never ridden a Chad in my life," Lana joked.

"You're riding a Jenny, remember?"

"Story of my life. Tali?"

I stopped untangling the bridle in my hand.

"Are you worried about that Safari stuff?"

I continued untangling. "Yes. That's why I think horses are a good plan. We can look for another map."

"Oh yeah, you gave my map away." She rolled her eyes.

I smiled. "Lana, we'll find another. It was the least we could do for them, for Mohamed."

"I liked those guys. Maybe we'll see them again on the roads. We'll have couple friends again."

"You can cook brunch for them when we see them."

"Also." She paused, her fingers stopping their work. "If the Safari have guns, does that mean we can find guns too?"

"Why would you want a gun, Lana?" My brow creased. She knew how to use a gun – she'd gone on a company away day to some countryside shooting range with one of her top clients. He taught her how to shoot a gun, tried to seduce her, was sorely disappointed at her lack of heterosexuality.

"Because if we see them, I want to be able to shoot them back." She mimed shooting, using a bridle as a rifle.

"Full of surprises, aren't you."

"And that is exactly why we're been married this long. I'm fresh, original. The original can't-make-up-her-mind queen. And you're my calm in a storm, my constant in a sea of variables."

"I guess we're looking for a farmhouse gunrack tonight then."

"Think the farmers are packing round here?" She grinned.

"Farmers. Farmer's mums." I continued her joke, her reference to a movie that probably no longer existed in its home nation.

"Oooh!" she burst. "I could be like Sargent Angel on that horse with all the guns at the end."

"I would love to watch a movie with you in some old farmhouse full of shotguns."

"You think they've got movies in Fort William?"

"I fucking hope so. If they've got a generator, then I'm getting a TV."

"I stopped paying our Netflix subscription though." She feigned innocence.

We laughed for the hour it took us to sort out the tack. We matched Chad's bridle to the bay, Jenny, at Lana's amusement. Sparkles was my Chester. Cinnamon, Tiger-Lilly, stayed bridleless, but she let me fit a saddle to her, and on it, I attached a bag of horse feed, some bits of equipment like a hoof pick and a spare girth. She was happy with that but shied away with any movement near her head. Maybe she had been hurt, maybe she had a bad experience with a person. I hoped not.

I mounted the bay first, adjusted the stirrups, tightened the girth. He was bombproof, like he had been the calmest horse in a previous life. He was perfect for Lana. I attached a lunge line to his bridle just in case and tied it to the saddle on Chester.

"Ready to ride?" I asked Lana.

She nodded, but her hands were tucked firmly inside her sleeves. I passed her the riding helmet I had found, the only one, and she placed it on her head. I did her chinstrap up, my fingers brushing across her milky soft skin. She was too nervous to recognise my flirting.

I held the stirrup steady. She put her left foot in.

"Hold on to the front of the saddle. On the count of three, jump up, and swing your other leg over Jenny."

She nodded, positioned herself.

"One, two, three!"

She jumped, swung her leg over Jenny, and landed perfectly in place. Her smile beamed, made the sun seem dimmer than before.

"I did it." She turned to me. "I did it, Tali."

"Because you're awesome. Look at you," I said.

I mounted Chester, he moved slightly as I swung over but I didn't falter. Lana seemed worried for a second, then her face returned to glee. Her knuckles were white where she held the reigns.

"Relax your hands, Lana. You won't need the reigns much with this guy. He seems to know his stuff."

"He's a damn fine beast, my Jenny." Seemed like most little girls got gooey over horses, even ones in their late thirties.

"Lana," I said.

Her face went serious. "Yes?"

"You look so fucking badass on horseback, I just want you to know."

"Yeah?" She looked down at herself in the saddle. "You liking this look?"

My cheeks ached at the smile that appeared on my face. My words, flowing freely, were landing despite her anxiety. "I like all your looks, babe. Ready to ride?"

She nodded, bit her lip. I kept Jenny close on the lunge line as I walked Chester from the courtyard out onto the country road that had led us here. Lana held on to the front of the saddle as she got used to the motion, but she soon eased up. Tiger-Lilly followed, nervous.

Bare tree branches covered the lane like a skyward cradle. The sun leaked through the gaps, splattering the path in front of us, covering Lana's face with golden freckles. I didn't feel like I was riding through the end of the world, I felt like I was riding through memories of her.

Tiger-Lilly was behind us, stopping to graze on what she could find in the hedgerow, but always keeping up with us, her new herd.

The horses were calm, carrying us like they knew they should, taking us to safety. In my mind, I promised Chester I would get him somewhere safe, maybe in Fort William he could have a paddock on the hills, spend the day grazing, drinking from streams. He felt narrow between my legs. His girth had to be tight, using the holes further down with the buckle. His withers were sunken, gaunt with a year of malnourishment. I had already become attached to the animals, not for what they were going to help us achieve, but for what they had already helped us achieve, a happiness in Lana I had not seen for some time.

"Cain would have loved this. He would have loved these fucking things." Lana closed her eyes. She seemed to rock like a new mother in the sun beams, letting Jenny take away her worries.

"You wanna talk about him for a bit?" I asked, tempting fate.

She looked over at me, lips straight, eyes still. "Yeah. I think we should."

I let my breath out. "Remember when he broke that plate and

36

said the wind blew it?"

She threw her head back in laughter. "We were fucking in-doors."

"He was not great at bullshitting."

"Neither are you. He gets that from you. Got that. Got that from you."

"I guess. Remember when he tripped on an actual banana peel?"

"Shit, yes. I could not stop laughing but he was crying. I felt like the worst mother in the world."

"You were the best mother in the world. The. Best. I fucking wished you were my mum half the time."

"Well, then we couldn't have fucked." She laughed. The shrill-ness unsettled the birds above our heads. They darted into the sky, little black pin pricks against the blue winter above.

"Do you think we'll find a shotgun?" she asked.

"I think we need to head west. Find some more rural land, cross England at its narrowest point. They'll have shotguns on the remote farms."

"If only we had a map," she teased.

"We're in Stanhope, in the Pennines. I'm looking for signs to Alston. Then from there we head north west to Brampton. There'll be signs to Gretna Green then."

"Oh, babe. Are we eloping again?"

"I fucking wish. I would marry you again."

"So would I. I hope you know that." Her gaze lingered.

I didn't. I felt like she was only with me now because she had to be. I chose my words, let them sound out in my head before I said them. "Sometimes I need reminding. But Greta Green is touristy. There'll be a ton of signs to get there. Once we're there, we know we can't go wrong. Follow the coast around like we said we would to Fort William."

"When did you get so good at navigating?"

"When we realised how hard maps were to find." I winked at her.

A fox bolted from one side of the road to the other. The horses froze, lifted their hooves and stamped.

"Natali, Tali?" Lana's hands were white on the saddle, her body lurching forwards.

"Woah. Woah there," I cooed to the horses. "Pull the reigns back a little. Let him know you're still there, still in control."

She did so, even cooed at him like I was doing.

"See? You got this," I said.

Jenny settled quickly, his hooves now firmly on the ground. Chester pulled at his bit, keen to move forward now his spook had dissipated. Tiger-Lilly stood far behind, watching with curious eyes. I dismounted, gestured for Lana to do the same.

"We need to run, don't we?" she asked, shakily coming down from Jenny.

"Yeah, think we do."

"I almost forgot about Sloth, Tali. I felt so normal, even on a horse. Felt like an expensive adventure holiday."

"Scared me, what Mohamed said about their friend, Sarah. She only forgot for five minutes."

"We're more careful than that, since Cain. You think they'll ever cure it?"

"That guy we met on the road a few weeks ago, the one who told us about Fort William, he said that all the global powerhouses, China, the US, said that they're working on cures for us."

She snorted. "Not for us, for them, in case it makes it over there. Last pandemic we had, it got out so quick. Good thing the airlines learned fast."

"That guy, he said they ran a fundraising event or something, like Comic Relief, or like Band Aid."

"Ha!" Lana laughed some more.

"What?"

"Band Aid. I get it now. Because music and plasters. We don't call them band aids here. It never made fucking sense to us. Can't be bloody Band Plasters, could it?"

I couldn't help it. I laughed. It was the perfect Lana moment. I felt Chester lean away from me as I doubled over and giggled. "Fuck's sake, Lana." I leaned in, took her giggling face in my hands, and kissed her. Her mouth took half a second to respond, but she kissed me back, passionately but ever so gracefully, like her lips were leading me in a ballroom dance. When we finished, we stared at each other for a while, my hand twiddling her hair. We were both remembering, remembering how we loved each other.

She laughed some more after a while, placed her fingers on her wrists. "Goal line," she said. "I just hit it."

I checked mine too. "Yep. Same. Maybe we should focus on laughing with each other then?" I raised an eyebrow. "Or kissing?"

"Tali, I'm trying."

I turned my head away from her.

"Please, you know how hard I'm trying, how hard I've always tried." She leaned to catch my eye.

"Lana – I know. I'm here. Just know that. Your laugh... I always need that."

She laughed some more, mockingly at first, testing my reaction, showing off like a kid. It echoed around the lanes ahead of us, and I swore for a second it made the branches shake above us. Her laugh was powerful; it always had been.

We walked, leading the horses for an hour or so to give them a break. We let them graze at patches of grass at the side of the lane, took their bits out so they could chew faster. They seemed happy, more relaxed than they'd been in that boggy field. Jenny kicked at an old wooden post to get to the grass underneath its straight edge.

"Jenny, dear? What have you found for me?" Lana said, crouching by the horse's head, with no fear. "Look, Tali. It's a sign."

"Like a sign from fate, or literally a sign?"

She turned. "It is literally a sign. See?" She brushed it off. Mud, dust and leaves crumbled from it. "Says 'Bolt Hole Farm. Second Right.'" She raised an eyebrow at me.

The mouse version of Lana rose in my mind. She turned into a lioness graced by golden sunlight. She grinned. Her canine's sharp points dripped with warmth, with light, with strength.

I'll admit, I was keen to find somewhere for us for the night. Not because I needed rest or to feed the horses, but because I wanted so badly to make love to Lana.

Bolt Hole Farm rested atop a hill overlooking a small town. It was nearly dark by the time we had settled the horses in a secure paddock outside; it was steep, so all the damp rested at the bottom of the hilly field. There was a small lake too. We walked down there before we had even looked inside the farmhouse.

We held hands watching the sun finally disappear, as the corpses of the farm's previous inhabitants sat on a bench overlooking the water, one head on the other's shoulder. Their flesh had rotted away, only scraps of clothes hung to their bones. They must have decided to die there, together, slowly fading into the unknown by each other's side. We felt bad about the whole Butt

Hole Farm thing after that.

The farmhouse door was unlocked. It opened to a kitchen, where all the cupboards were open above avocado tiles and MDF surfaces. There was a breakfast bar in the middle of the room. Lana sat at it, picked up a piece of paper stained with a coffee cup ring.

"Dear guests," she started. "Take what you need. Stay for as long as you need. Sloth has taken us both. We all pay for the sins of our past. This is God's reckoning on our small country. God's reckoning on the sinners, the sodomites, the murderers and adulterers. When Sloth is done, what next? Will we suffer for our pride, our greed, for lust, envy, gluttony and our wrath? Our Father, who art in heaven –"

"Yeah, you don't need to read the whole thing, Lana, I know how this goes."

"Dammit, I thought these two would be decent. Bet they're turning in their graves with two lesbians staying in their house."

"They're not in a grave."

"It feels like people go either one of two ways when something shitty happens. They either reject religion or take to it with more gusto than ever."

"Yeah, well we didn't take it that seriously at the start."

I took to the cupboards. Lana took to looking for her elusive shotgun. There wasn't much. A bag of flour, some yeast. I took the flour, yeast, placed it on the breakfast bar. I started to tidy. People had come through here like locusts, taking advantage of the hospitality shared by the suffering, not cleaning up the discarded wrappers, plastic.

I remembered meals we shared at the start of Sloth. We sat at our round table, Cain sitting on a cushion because he was too big

41

for his child seat, too small for a proper seat. He had just turned six. Lana told him that people were getting poorly on an island in the sea. He asked if we could go to help them. We treated this virus, disease, like it was any other false-start epidemic. Like bird flu, and mad cow disease before it. Some people panicked, but the majority of people had faith that the government would protect us, like Lana and I. It was more than an inconvenience this time.

When the looting started, we left London, rented an Airbnb on the outskirts of Surrey to be safe, not from the disease, but from worried people. We watched the news for longer and longer each day waiting for a safe time to return. It never came. When the first reported case surfaced in the countryside, we wished we had prepared more. The last ever headline from the media was RUN. WE'VE ALL GOT IT ALREADY. And then the country went silent.

Each day after that we saw fewer and fewer people on the roads. Our car was stolen a week after the last headline. We felt stranded, exposed. Lana suggested we take to the roads ourselves after I came back empty handed from the smashed-up Tesco Express. She said that if we had become looters, we may as well move around, finding new places to get food and supplies like 'a proper apocalypse'. She said that if the media had shut down, Murdoch was probably dead, and the army would come soon. Turns out, the army was affected as badly as everyone else, and Murdoch was not dead, but on lock-down with the rest of the elite, protected, with a special drug that had been in development for longer than Sloth had actually existed. Lana said Sloth was the perfect storm for pharmaceuticals and the elite to scratch each other's backs.

It was harder at the start, making Cain understand why it was important to run around every three hours. Alarms never woke him, only Lana's voice did. She kept him on her running time-table. I'd sometimes watch as they jogged, hand in hand, through fields, down lanes, across carparks, his little legs trying so hard to keep up with her. He enjoyed it, but not when he was tired. In the end, that was his downfall.

I slammed my fist on the countertop. The bag of flour toppled over, spilling over the floor I had just cleared. I cursed, wiped a tear from my eye. I had always been the less-emotional one, not because I was cold, but because Lana was so emotional, there had never been any room for me. I heard her footsteps coming down the stairs. I grabbed a mixing bowl, it took me a few attempts to find one, then I collected all the flour in, added water from my bottle and began to knead, over and over and over again like it would bring Cain back.

"Look what I found," Lana said, coming into the kitchen.

I expected a shotgun, but it was a Band Aid CD. A tear rolled down my face as I laughed. I wiped it away, but Lana saw.

She took a step towards me, looked at the dough in my hands. "Is that gluten free?"

I laughed again, then her arms were around me, thin ropes of warmth that smelled like everything I had ever loved in my life. She nestled her head into my neck. Her breathing made the hair on my neck stand up.

"Tali, it's been a good day," she whispered.

"I know."

She kissed me, made a dirty joke about raising our heartrates upstairs. I led her up there, following her directions through a smile I wanted to catch, bottle, and savour forever.

I lay her down on the bed. A cloud of dust ejected into the air. She mock coughed and pulled me down on top of her. I kissed

43

every bare inch of her before she flipped me over and took control. I felt like we were in our twenties again, free, wild, intoxicated by each other, always wanting, needing each other's flesh.

When she took her jumper off, her shirt, and the T shirt under that, my heart dropped at how thin she had become. She had never been a curvy woman, but now, her body was a map of ridges and ribs, all showing through thin pale skin. Her breasts had shrunk too, her skin looked strained, like it had lost it elasticity. She was beautiful, my Gaia in a world where ribs showed, skin was tired, and minds twisted.

We touched, kissed every morsel of skin on each other's body. She came first, me shortly after. Seeing her climax was my drug of choice. It wound the coil in my body so tightly that when it broke, I was in heaven, drifting slowly downwards like the first brown leaf of late summer. There was a calm after that, a peace we settled in, naked, hearts over the goal line. We fell asleep. Our alarms didn't wake us. The sound of gunfire did.

T

I pressed my face against the dark cold window. Lana sat on the edge of the bed, sheets tucked around her waist. Pockets of light flashed in the valley below the hill, the small town that looked up to where we were. She became the mouse again in my mind, shy, bewildered, hiding from the predatory world.

"Is it fireworks?" she asked. I was sure she knew what it really was.

"Gunfire. Down in that town. We're safe here. No lights, okay?"

"You think it's the same guys from before?"

"I don't know, Lana. But I have heard more gun fire in the past week than in my entire lifetime."

She nodded. I continued to watch the blackness, specks of white gold rippling from it. It went quiet for a few minutes. All I could hear was Lana breathing behind me. The bed creaked as she got up, let the sheet fall to the floor. She rested her head on my shoulder from behind, peering into the blackness with me. The gunfire started up again. We both jumped at the sound.

"Should we leave?" she whispered like her voice would carry to them.

"I don't know, Lana. Maybe we should check on the horses, see if they're spooked."

"I don't wanna go out there, honey."

I turned, pulled her in close to me. "Let's just get dressed, pack up, be ready. We'll leave at dawn." I lifted her head with one hand, stroked her bottom lip with my thumb. Another bout of gunfire echoed across the hills from the town below.

I worked in the kitchen most of the night in darkness, separating balls of dough into Ziplock bags to take on the road.

"There was a workshop on the side of the house. I found tea bags next to the kettle in there. These too." Lana stood in the doorway with a hammer and a crowbar. "I think we should arm ourselves."

"I agree. I think we should have done that a while back. We've been lucky."

"Or naïve," she replied. "Which one?"

"Hammer," I said. The crowbar would give Lana a better range. "No gun then?"

"Not here. But we'll find one, love. Make sure we can defend ourselves if we need to. I'm not saying they'll come up here, but I want to be prepared."

"If it wasn't for Mohamed, I think we might have died."

"I do, too." She stared for a moment, a tenseness rising up her body, making itself known in little ticks and twitches. She smiled a little, just enough to hide her fear.

"The country is in ruins, most of the people are dead, and we've still got idiots going around causing trouble."

She reached out her dainty hand. "You made me feel a little stronger when they were above us, just a little, but it helped. I liked the horses too. Didn't think I would."

"All white women like horses."

"You can't white shame a lesbian." She smiled, but it faded quickly. "I am scared, though, honey. Sloth is tough enough, but that Safari stuff, it's haunting me. I just don't understand how it's a game to some people."

"It's getting to me too. I want to get to Fort William as soon as we can. I just want to be safe, not wake up panicked in the middle of the night. I want to have a shower, eat something real. I want to rest, truly rest, without my ears picking up the slightest sound in the wind."

"I'd like that, too. With you." She slipped the crowbar into her backpack so it stuck out slightly. She practised reaching it and readjusted it so it was accessible. I pushed the hammer in my belt.

"I'm gonna feed the horses now."

"Alone?"

"Yeah. I'll be fine. Just need to get them fed before we leave when the sun comes up. Stay here."

The darkness lingered in the air like a ghostly fog. The horizon lightened; the gunfire had stopped. In its place, several columns of smoke rose from the town, silhouetted against the dark grey sky. I could smell the burning. It mixed with the scent of damp, late winter air.

I climbed over a fence in the courtyard to the field we had given to the horses. They were idlily standing close by, tails flicking, the occasional snort coming from them. I called to them quietly. Jenny and Chester responded, slowly walked to me and the feed. Tiger-Lilly stayed back, but her nostrils flared at the scent of molasses.

I knelt in the mud to split it evenly between them. My head bolted up as I heard the strained breaths of something, someone. I turned to the house, no Lana. I focused my eyes in the darkness, frozen on my haunches behind Jenny as he nibbled at the feed.

A faint outline of a small man, no, child, emerged from darkness and fog. His left arm covered his right. His steps were jagged, swaying from side to side. My breathing increased. My nostrils flared. Eyes widened.

"Psssst!" I called through the dark. I was sure the kid heard me, his speed increased. "Quick! Here at the horses!"

My hands dropped into the mud, steadying myself. I dug my fingertips into the ground, each one meeting the chill of the earth. He must have been a survivor of the attack on the town. His outline got clearer and clearer in the dark. He had blonde hair, was no older than nine or ten. His clothes were torn, no backpack, no weapon, not even shoes. He tripped. My heart stopped. There was a long moment of silence, only the noises from the horses echoed in the air.

I saw an elbow, then a head, and soon the boy was back on his feet. I urged him on, desperate for him to come to me, so I could save him, give him the chance Cain never had. His breathing became louder. He was nearly safe, nearly in my arms.

I crawled forwards, my knees sinking into mud. I slid slightly, picked up momentum against the wet slope. The child darted, fell into my arms.

"He's coming! The man, the posh man!" The kid's voice was loud, piercing almost. I was worried the shooter would get us, but more worried we would lead him to Lana.

I shushed him.

He continued to sob, shaking each sound out of his mouth with fear.

"Honey, be quiet." I pulled him in. My lips rested against his damp hair. "On three, we're gonna run to the top of the field, scoot under the fence and run to a shed on the left. You know your lefts and rights?"

"What about the man? The bald man. He speaks posh."

"That's why we gotta run."

I felt him nod against me. I counted as he gripped onto me. When I got to three, I darted. He didn't. His hand pulled me back.

"Honey, please. You have to run with me. Shall I carry you?"

"No, I can do it, lady. I can run."

I gripped his hand tighter. I pulled him, felt his arm nearly come clean out of his socket, but his body responded. He started to run with me.

We reached the fence as we heard commotion at the bottom of the field, splashes in water, mud; the splashes of many boots. I flipped onto my back and rolled under the fence, turned to pull the boy through.

A gunshot rang out across the steep field. He fell instantly, his head face down in the mud, an elbow stuck at an odd angle resting on the bottom rung of the fence.

"Ten!" I heard echo through the field, the same voice we heard from beneath the bridge.

I screamed but clapped my hand across my mouth before it rang into the night's air. I wretched. Bile came from my mouth, my empty stomach trying to purge the horror from my body. I sobbed for the boy, for Cain, for the crack appearing in my heart. I threw my head back, wiped my mouth and edged away from the fence, knowing there was nothing more I could do. I crawled in the mud, tears running down my face, dripping onto my hands, my dreadlocks dragging in the sodden filth. I couldn't catch my breath. I turned to check for danger.

There was no sound from the dark field, no sound from the valley below. I was panting, not with exhaustion, but with grief. I edged parallel to the fence, to where the horses lingered in the corner, startled by everything.

I unlatched the gate to the field, let it swing open. The horses followed me as I crawled to the shed where we had stored their saddles. Once inside, I felt no relief, no respite from the fear, anxiety. I wasn't done yet. Would they come for the boy's body? I had to get her away from them too.

I saddled the horses up in silence, only sobs breaking through. I wiped away tears that were for the little boy, and Cain, made sure they never dropped onto the rugged leather on the horse's backs. It felt like hours, but it was seconds before they were ready to go. I led the two, Tiger-Lilly following, to the door to the farmhouse. I opened it, still holding on to the horses, and gestured to Lana, pulling on her jumper.

"What happened?" she shouted.

"Lana, no. Be quiet. They're close, they're really close," I sobbed. "We need to go. I need you to get on Jenny now and we need to disappear. Please, please, babe. Do what I say. When we're further away, I'll tell you what happened." My words, so desperate to be free without a care for how they sounded, how they were received, bled from me like the wound in the little boy's back.

"I heard a gunshot. Are you hurt?" She looked up and down my body.

"No. Not shot. Someone tried to but missed," I lied. I didn't want to share my trauma with her, she didn't deserve the pain of seeing a child murdered.

She nodded, tightened her pack up and mounted Jenny.

We rode in complete silence through the dawn. My voice lost all its bravery, my words lost all their confidence. The damp air damp lost its crispness as the sun rose. The roads I chose were empty, single-tracked lanes that were now overgrown with hedgerow species and nettles. Birds sang. Pheasants ran panicked in front of us till they found spots to disappear into the hedges. An hour into the morning, she looked at me.

I exhaled. My breath shuddered as it escaped. My words were timid, scared of being free. "I was feeding the horses. Someone was at the bottom of the field. They shot at me. That's it. They didn't come after me, but I got out there quick."

She didn't respond but her eyes had a new glassiness to them, like frustrated tears were sealing her inside her own mind. The birds sang, some so loud it jarred my ears.

"Will we make it to Brampton today?" she asked after some time.

"I was thinking we could get further."

"Gretna?"

"Yeah. It's forty miles from here, but we'll have to cross the M6. I want you to practise going faster on Jenny, so we can get across there quick."

She patted Jenny on the neck. "I think we can do that. Huh, Jenny?" She turned to me. "He said he'd look after me." She smiled, I think more for me than her, and tussled Jenny's mane. "If Cain was still with us, I would have let him have Jenny. I would have had your Chester, and you would have had to brave Tiger-Lilly."

"You been thinking about that?"

"I think about Cain every second of every day. I weave him into whatever we do, imagine what he would do in situations. I imagined he'd like Mo, and Daniel and Ryan. I knew he'd like the horses. That, along with you, was what got me in the saddle. He'd like those dough balls you've been cooking on the fire."

"Damn, that boy loved gluten." We both laughed. "Lana, tell me more. Tell me how he would have been now." My voice trembled with sentiment.

51

Her lips straightened. She licked them, easing up the dryness. "He would have shot up. He'd be like nearly your height now."

"Well, that's not hard."

"It's his seventh birthday in the spring. Think I would have tried to track down some Star Wars toy for him, but took out the batteries so it wouldn't give me a headache. He would have cheered when I found that map, cheered even harder when we got that chocolate. I'm saving it, Tali. I'm saving it for his birthday. It was only a Freddo, and now it's the most valuable fucking thing we own."

I wondered if Cain would have stayed happy with this kind of life, or if he would have quietened, grew solemn like his mother. Maybe the world wouldn't have made him cheer anymore. But maybe, if he was still here with us, Lana would have stayed clear of the depression that held her captive now, and neither one of us would have ever felt the weight of Sloth. It was so heavy, like we were sea creatures trying to move on land, heavy with fear, with listlessness, with the routine you stuck to or else you died. I wanted to move, shed the slow, shed the heavy.

"You wanna trot for five? You can sit in the saddle, that's called a sitting trot, like what the cowboys do. Or you can move up and down with the trot, that's a rising trot, it'll be less bumpy because you're a part of the movement."

"Like being in a boat verses being in the sea?" She couldn't have known how much her metaphor resonated with me.

"Yes, exactly. Just hold onto the saddle till you're sure. Then make sure your heels are down, you sit back in the saddle, straight, and go up and down with the rhythm."

She raised an eyebrow. "Like fucking a man."

"I wouldn't know."

"I wish I didn't."

I gave Chester a gentle kick in his sides. He immediately picked up his pace and I rose with his trot. I gestured to Lana to do the same. Jenny burst into a trot quite abruptly. It knocked Lana's helmet to the bridge of her nose. She gripped the saddle with one hand, straightened it up with the other and tried to rise. She was out of rhythm, bouncing in and out of the saddle with little control. I started to count out loud, slowed Chester down to trot at the same pace as Jenny. Lana understood music, she understood a beat and timing. I counted in fours, exaggerating the twos and the fours to encourage her to rise on those beats.

In an hour, she was cantering down dirt roads. Tiger-Lilly had started to run ahead of us instead of behind. She was growing more confident, convinced that maybe we were her new herd. We started seeing signs to Greta Green and our hearts raced like the beasts beneath us. We let the horses walk for the next hour; they had grown sluggish from the exercise. When we emerged from countryside into the outer town reaches of Brampton, we stopped to rest.

Lana spread out her coat like a picnic blanket. It was a coat that mainly stayed wrapped around her waist. We let the horses roam a small school playing field as we watched from the side lines like supportive football mums. We checked the locker rooms for stopwatches first. There were none.

"Think Cain would have got any sportier?" I asked Lana.

"Fuck no; that boy watched The Greatest Showman far too many times."

"Ah. That's why he asked me why I didn't have a beard. I just thought he had finally realised he didn't have a dad."

"Two mums trump a nuclear family anyway. We tried far harder to have him than any straight couple."

I passed her some bread I had cooked on an open fire that

morning, quickly, efficiently whilst the horses took a break. She tore at it, picking at it like she wasn't hungry. "Look, the ponies are sleeping."

The horses lay together at the edge closest to us, like they thought we were all having a nap together. "Our herd." I chewed at bread. "What was that thing you kept saying to Cain? The light, the fire?"

"Ah. That he was a fire that would burn in the rain, or a light that would never go out."

"He took that literally, you know?"

"Yeah, I know." She looked to the sky, to the horses. "Guess that was bullshit too."

"We better cross that motorway soon." I took my pulse. "After a quick run." I offered her my hand, pulled her up. We ran around the school field once, the horses opening the occasional eye to check on us. After I caught my breath, I called to the horses. They raised their heads, flicked their tails, but didn't come to me. I turned to look at Lana; she was already looking back at me with curiosity.

I called to them again. They seemed to strain. I bent to the pile where our saddles and packs were stacked on the overgrown grass and pulled out the nearly empty bag of molasses.

"Come," I called to them, shaking the bag. Tiger-Lilly rose first, walking calmly to me and took molasses from my hands, her first sign of trust. The other two slowly stood, shaking at the ankles. I called them again, encouraging them along. Chester neared me, lent his ginger head against my side. I offered him food. He took it, chewed slowly.

"What's wrong with them?" Lana asked, her eyes wide.

"Maybe they're just tired," I said.

"But what if they're not?"

"Just say it, Lana."

"Sloth. What if they have Sloth?"

"I don't know if it affects animals."

"Exactly. Their metabolism is all different to ours. What if they got it without us realising?"

"Lana, we've all got it."

"No, we've all got the virus, but its dormant till we slow. Like HIV and AIDS. HIV doesn't turn into AIDS right away. Maybe their goal line is different to ours. Natali, what if it's the opposite for them? Making their heart faster makes the virus active?"

"Lana, they're just tired. They've been stuck in a field for a year." I took her hand; it didn't respond to my touch. The broken side of her was emerging again, that irate, shrill part, her anxiety and her depression all in one.

"What if they were scared before, so their heart rates never dropped enough, but now they're with us, they're more relaxed, so the Sloth kicked in?"

"Lana, please." I fumbled at Chester's mane.

"What if – "

"Lana, stop." I took my hand away from hers. I held Chester by the headcollar, fastened his bit, and did the same to Jenny. "We need to cross that motorway before it gets dark."

I thrust the reins of both horses into her chest, told her to hold them while I saddled up. She didn't speak a word, not even when Chester rubbed against her arm for affection. I felt like an illusion had shattered into tiny pieces of stale happiness on a desolate ground.

"Are we ready to go now?" she asked as I mounted Chester.

"Yes."

She mounted Jenny. The horse's legs wobbled as Lana's meagre weight was added, but Jenny started to walk forward with

55

Chester and I. Tiger-Lilly did her own thing but stayed closer than before.

As we trotted on cracked concrete roads through residential areas and industrial estates, the horses became fearful, unsure of their steps. They were slowing, very gradually, but I couldn't muster up the thought that they may be sick. Lana's lips were straight, her eyes wide. Every stumble Jenny made, Lana flinched, laying a hand on his withers.

We encountered the survivors from the shooting the night before. One man, a bullet hole in his gut saturating his clothes, lay on the back of a cart as three people pulled him. They all stopped when they saw us, raised their pointy sticks at us.

"We won't hurt you," I said.

They reacted by falling to their knees, sobbing.

I dismounted, approached them with palms raised. "What happened?"

A woman, slight, shaking like the increasing wind would blow her over, looked up at me. "There was an attack. Group of people in suits on the back of trucks. They lit our entire community up. Made us run for them, like target practice."

"You got away," Lana said.

"Only us. My father can't run now. He hasn't run since last night. The Sloth will get him before the wound will."

"You can come with us," I burst. My stomach lurched, a vein in my forehead throbbed. The memory of the sound of the boy falling to the damp earth echoed in me, made my fingers weak, my fists loose. "We're heading to Fort William, in the mountains. We can be safer there."

"We thought we were safe in that valley. We couldn't even fight back against the guns."

Another man spoke. "It was like when the natives met the

colonists. We had no chance."

"Come with us. Come north to the hills. We can work on protection; we know about them now." My voice shook with urge.

The woman shook her head, wiped a tear away. "We have to let Dad die first."

"Then we'll stay, wait for you."

Lana moved closer to me, held my hand to show her support.

"We'll wait," she whimpered to them.

The woman nodded. A tear flew through the air and landed on the tarmac. An arm raised from the cart and gripped the side. An elderly man struggled to pull himself up. His eyes appeared from the cart, but he could go no further.

"No," he whispered, not like he was trying to keep quiet, but like he could not summon the volume. "You two need to go. I won't let you delay your journey for a dying man, not when you've still got each other." His head fell back as soon as his words had left his lips. His daughter lay a hand on his forehead, her lip quivering, her eyes darting around her father's face.

We left them shortly after. I told them the way north. Lana taught them how to take their heart rates manually. The old man listened, unable to participate, unable to resist his body shutting down, but he thanked us quietly for the gift we left with his family. He said he could die now; he knew they would be a little wiser, a little safer than before.

"It's okay, isn't it?" he said to us both, his family out of earshot. "It's okay for me to love another man, isn't it?"

Lana's eyebrows furrowed.

"It's gonna be okay in heaven. If they sent me angels that are gay, I know it's okay for me to be. I loved a man once, that was the eighties though. I hope he knows its okay. I hope he met people like you before he died, just so he knew what we did wasn't wrong."

After an hour of walking, silently, the deathbed coming-out keeping us quiet, thoughtful, we stopped outside a corner shop with its door swinging wide open. I dismounted. Chester swayed. Lana dismounted, but didn't come inside with me. The ground inside the shop crunched. Behind the counter, I found a map of Scotland, spread out, open like it wanted me to find it.

A corpse leant up against the wall, a shotgun in its embrace.

I gasped at first, inhaling the vile sweetness of death, and gagged. I pulled my jacket over my mouth and nose and lifted the gun carefully, scared it would go off. I lay it on the counter, convinced it wasn't sentient. I dropped to my knees and fumbled in the drawers under the counter, moving the frail legs of the corpse. Under stacks of receipt paper rolls, I found a box of shotgun cartridges. A smile warmed my face, waiting to reveal itself to Lana. I thought it might refresh her positivity. I bundled up the gun, its barrel facing towards the ground, and tucked the cartridges and map under my arm.

I stalled, spotting Lana outside. She had Jenny's head close to her mouth, whispering in the animal's ear. My chest went heavy. My breath burst from me, along with a solitary tear I had battled to keep from the world. She had the same look as when she realised Cain had symptoms.

He wouldn't get up one night to run, despite Lana urging him to, begging him, like her tears would make him. We were sleeping in a car that night. It was an old Landrover. I hated them normally, but they were comfortable, gave us a height advantage. When Cain didn't wake, his face was lit with Lana's torchlight. Her heartrate was raised beyond anything a run could have achieved, and yet, he moaned, batted us away, told us he was too tired now.

Lana's voice went croaky, strained by her pleading, her desperation. We didn't leave that car with Cain ever again. We spent the three days it took him to die trying to figure out where we had gone wrong, if we had missed something, if he hadn't run as fast as he had always done by Lana's side. We couldn't work it out. So, we wept. We kissed his head, played with his hair, until he could barely breathe.

That's when Lana asked me to kill him.

She lay her head against his as I plunged the blunt knife into the back of his skull. We discussed for hours before that we would do it this way, straight into the brain, lights out. She whimpered as she heard the cracking of his skull, sobbed when she felt his blood slowly leak out. She stayed with his body for another two days after that. We buried him in an orchard and barely spoke for a month after. I was consumed with the hate I felt for myself. Lana was just consumed.

Through the shards of broken glass hanging loosely from the window frame of the corner shop, Lana's face, her movements, were much like when Cain had gotten sick. The sky was darkening overhead. Clouds moved fast. The air seemed to chill as I walked outside.

Lana half smiled at the sight of the gun, but thunder erupted over her head. The horses didn't flinch; they just swayed on the spot, tired, slow. The sound of birds stopped. A single drop of rain hit Lana's cheek. She wiped it away, looking at her fingers like the rain was unwelcome on her flesh.

"A shotgun?" she asked, her voice raised slightly over the sound of thunder.

"Ammo too, and a map." I looked up as a bolt of lightning crossed the sky. "We better get moving."

"Honey, I don't think the horses can." Lana went back to Jenny's mane, twiddling it with her fingers.

I passed her the shotgun, tucked the cartridges in her backpack, and kissed her on the cheek. "Let's get them to Gretna Green."

"But if they're sick?"

There was no doubt in my mind. "They just need to rest," I lied.

The sky turned unnaturally dark. Lightness flickered across the desolate motorway, a haunting concrete river separating us from safety. Cars littered the six lanes and central partition, all grey with dust and debris. Vans lay on their sides, their contents spilled out on to the tarmac. Litter blew in the increasing winds, darting, floating from bonnet to boot, skipping over lanes and down the hard shoulder. Lightning plagued the sky and grew closer with every bolt. Rain splattered unevenly but picked up frequency as we sat on horseback. The horses didn't react to the weather, to the rain, to the thunderstorm raging above.

"We're going to have to canter, jump over the central reservation. Just remember to lean forward when Jenny jumps. He'll do it. He'll lead the way."

Lana pulled her coat up around her neck, straightened the strap of the shotgun which now rested at her waist, more like a satchel bag than a deadly weapon. Her fist was white, gripping onto Jenny's saddle horn, but her fingers rested on his withers, moving like she was playing piano on him, comforting him. A bolt of lightning erupted across the sky. Lana flinched, but the horses didn't.

"Let's go," I called over the thunder.

I kicked at Chester's side. He didn't move. I kicked again. He took one step onto the tarmacked road, pawed at the ground with his hoof. I knew that sign. He wanted to lie down. I kicked him, harder this time. He took two more steps. His ankles gave way. I got my feet out of the stirrups just in time and jumped from him as he crashed to the cold wet road.

"Tali?" Lana cried.

I stood, checked myself for injuries. Chester twitched at my feet. I knelt by his head, ran my palm across his chestnut coat. Lana dismounted Jenny. He pawed at the ground, stepped into the first lane of the motorway, and lowered himself down.

"Tali, they are sick. I told you." Lana erupted into tears like the storm above our heads. "I fucking told you."

"I fucking KNOW, Lana!" I screamed. It echoed, made my heart race.

She ignored me, knelt at Jenny's side. Jenny pushed his head into Lana. She reacted by wrapping her arms around him, but he pushed her again, pushed and pushed till she fell back, telling her to run.

A gunshot rang out across the road. It echoed from steel cars, concrete, clouds above. At first, I thought Lana fired the shotgun to put Jenny out of his misery, but soon, the dim afternoon was exposed to the brightest clinical white. A flood light rained down on us. We both shielded our eyes.

"Lana! Run!" I cried, my voice snapping like it would break.

She stumbled to her legs, weak with grief. Her shoulders shook, her knuckles white. Each flash of lightning was drowned out by the flood lights.

An engine revved. We finally moved. Lana dashed to me, grabbing my hand as she neared. I led her, low to the ground, behind a toppled-over van in the far-right northbound lane. We were wedged between the central reservation and the van. The engine revved again. We heard something hit the tarmac. Then footsteps between each bout of thunder.

"Come out, come out wherever you are!" His familiar voice, southern, what I would have called a BBC accent, got quieter. "Boys, we got two five pointers here. Who hasn't scored today?"

A second set of footsteps grew closer. The clicking of a gun rattled to our ears. I turned to Lana. Tears streaked down her pale cheeks. Her eyes, facing up to the storm, were wide but focused. Her lips moved like she was talking to herself.

"They know we're here," I whispered. "We have to run for it." I took a look across the other side of the motorway. There was nothing for cover, no cars we could dart behind. I looked to the dark bodies that lay on the left lane, Jenny and Chester. They were still alive, Jenny more so than Chester. They would die on that lane, slowly, like they were drifting into a painful sleep. Tiger-Lilly was nowhere to be seen, she clearly had better sense than us.

"Lana, we're gonna run. Get ready," I whispered to her, readjusting my grip on her pale hand.

"Come on out, ladies! Not terribly sporting of you to hide!" the BBC accent called.

"How many do you think there are?" Lana's words shook.

"I don't know. Wait." A third set of footsteps joined them, and a fourth, with a hard slam. Four of them now on the ground, away from their truck.

"Boys, they're behind that van. We could blow it or hunt them on foot."

"Foot," one man said, accent similar. "Need more intact bodies to take back and it isn't terribly entertaining when we win so easily."

A laugh rang out, so forced it could be heard against the

thunder. Lana froze, her fingers pressed into her palm, my palm. I took her face, made her look me in the eye.

"I love you, Lana Novykova-Smith." Her pale hands rose to my cheeks too. She leaned her head on mine.

"I love you, my love, my Tali. I fucking love you."

I stood, darted over the central reservation, leading the way for Lana. There was a gunshot. I turned.

Lana stood in front of the four men. Her stance was spread, her gun raised with the power of a goddess. One had fallen, one had his arms raised, his shiny tuxedo glinting in the light. Lana shot again, just once, striking two more men in one. They fell. One writhed on the ground, the other gurgled like he was drowning.

"Lana!" I called as lightning streaked above our heads. My stomach pulled at me, urged me to scoop her up, or run, or something that wasn't just standing in a storm as my wife pointed a gun at someone. I took a step towards her.

A muscular arm circled around my neck pressing into my soft throat. The cool of metal throbbed against my temple. My hands shot up to the arm, nails dug into the flesh.

"Now, now, little lady. Why don't you settle down?" a woman whispered in my ear. Her voice was soft, like a grandmother telling a bedtime story. I couldn't see her, but I felt the silk she wore caress my figure, tickling at my ankles where her dress spread out in an A-line skirt. There was no way of knowing in that moment, but I bet the dress was red.

"Get your hands off me," I growled.

Her lips pressed against my other temple. "You rats sure are getting trickier to exterminate. Had a few more fight back this week, but I'm still winning. I'm the only woman on the leader board."

I struggled more but she held me like a scruffed cat, in control, rendering me useless against her grip. Red hair cascaded across my throat from behind.

She kicked the back of my leg, forcing me forward, toppling over the barrier back into the left side of the motorway. I scrambled, turning myself over, ignoring the gash pouring sticky warmth across my forehead. I reached for the hammer. The woman elegantly climbed atop of the central partition and jumped down onto my chest. The wind was knocked out of me like an accordion. My hand flexed like it was trying to capture the air my lungs had lost. I saw Lana turn to look at me as the women pulled me back up by my hair and placed her gun to my head.

The other man, with the voice we had been haunted by, backed away from Lana, white palms exposed, rain soaking his balding head. She reached into her backpack, reloaded the shotgun with precision, like she had been practising.

"Now, now, lady. We were only playing. Get a little stir crazy locked up away from the real world now, and we've work to do," he said. "The nerds need fresh samples back in the labs. Points mean prizes. We bring the bodies as young and fresh as we can get, they give us with the drugs." His face took on a sickly smile.

"Young bodies?" She spat as she repeated his words.

"See, younger hosts cure Sloth naturally, every few hours when we raise our heart rate. But as soon as it's gone, we get reinfected. It's in the air, in the water. Spores. As soon as Sloth finally stops your heart, your body releases it into the air. It's playing a game with us, always has been. The lab, need the samples – they're on to something. They're gonna isolate the thing that cures Sloth every time –"

"It's a protein," the red head interrupted.

"Isolate it, and replicate into a therapy for those who can't run and to stop reinfection. The rest of the game we do for fun, raise our own heartrates naturally. Killing two birds…" He smiled. "With one stone."

The woman who held me pushed me forward, urging me to the centre of the action. She smelled of lily of the valley.

"This isn't okay. This isn't right. For fun?" Lana barked. Her head jerked towards me. "And you thought it'd be okay to lay your hands on her? My wife? We are not your points. We are not your samples."

It might have been a second, but it felt like a lifetime. I pushed backwards into my captor, got away from her for a split moment, turned to Lana as she pulled the trigger.

When my head turned back, the redhead dropped to the ground, her face as crimson as her hair, her teeth exposed, lightning reflecting off them like a spotlight in a theatre show, the backdrop was the flesh that lay under her skin. She twitched a couple of times before she became still. Strands of her hair glittered when the lightning rang across the sky, highlighting the grey that had been concealed by temporary dye.

I wanted to run to Lana, take her hand and make her disappear with me, but I was caught in a moment of pride and fear. Lana was lit by the truck, her slender silhouette stretching across the motorway, only disappearing when lightning above lit the afternoon. Her hair dripped like a russet waterfall on white cliffs. Her stance, like she was Gaia, a warrior goddess, a lioness.

"Why don't you put the gun down, honey?" the man said.

"Don't you fucking call me honey," she scowled.

"We can work this out. We can give you the drugs, you won't have to run around like little mice anymore. You can be one of us, safe, protected, stimulated."

"It's too late for that. Down with the patriarchy," she muttered as she shot the man in the crotch. His scream, far higher than any woman I had fucked, echoed longer than the thunder. He lay writhing on the ground, clutching his junk.

The truck they were in, some kind of army issued one, rocked as a man, the driver, got out of the front. He came round the side, arms raised, Adam's apple slowly rising and sinking. Lana raised her gun to him.

"I'm just their driver!" he winged.

I joined Lana, carefully stepping over wet tarmac, full of pride, awe for her. Her side was where I belonged. "You think this is okay?" I barked at the driver.

"No! But I need their drugs! We got a babe. She's tiny. Can't make her run. Not all of us can run. Please!"

I have to admit I wanted Lana to kill him, end his life so he couldn't deliver the Safari to their hunting grounds ever again, but she lowered the gun.

"Lana, let's go. We need to go," I pleaded. Lana was still, her eyes so firmly on the driver she might have turned him to stone. I pulled at her arm.

She raised the gun again, shot the man in the right leg at the knee. Blood sprayed through the air, joined the raindrops hammering down from above. He didn't screech, he whimpered.

"You can hold your baby, but you can't drive those cunts anywhere again." She lowered the gun, pointed it at the BBC man who looked up at her, tears cascading down his face, and she reloaded. "This world gets a daily dose of fresh bodies without you picking on the living."

Then, she shot the men that lay beside him, making sure she had killed them cleanly before she turned the gun to him again, reloaded a final time, and pulled the trigger whispering I win. She was calmer in that moment than I had ever seen her. Her eyes darted to movement far beyond the truck. Spectators? Their footsteps pounded on wet concrete as they fled. Lana's face was stoic. She was silent till the steps were faint in the night.

She grabbed my hand, moved her gun back to her shoulder, and left the scene. Once she pulled me over the barriers of the other side of the road, she wept. She didn't stop weeping until we were a mile from the motorway.

H

We walked all night, quiet on hooves, searching for the sea, avoiding all. We dodged whispers in the dark that came from our minds, shadows in bushes crawling from our shaking souls, and specks of blood that had dried on our faces. We took it in turns to run. Lana went off on her own a few times. I heard her cry under trees, in deserted houses, in puddles littering the tarmac to the north. The lioness turned back into mouse.

We encountered another couple on the road, but Lana simply bared her gun and they left us alone. They shivered in fear like we had only hours before.

We smelled it first, then heard it. Each wave that crashed on unseen shores moved us on, yearning, wanting something so simple. She held my hand when we first saw the ocean, only for a moment. Her eyes closed as a breeze brought her lungs the rich salty air. I wanted to reach out and touch her face. The gloaming had always looked good on her. Pale skin made her eyes deep, the minimal light focusing on flesh rather than brown irises.

When the sun rose high on the Solway Coast, we found a huge house, a mansion, I guess. Tiger-Lilly followed us like a ghost all night, her head low, only looking up to make sure we were still there. She stood on the porch of the house, rubbing her head against the stone wall, scratching an itch that must have plagued her for miles. Lana and I both pushed the door open, our hands meeting on the rotting wood. It had become warped, damp, and had expanded. When we were inside, the light disappeared. Lana called out to the house, to check for other people. The mansion was clear, but not clean. The place was shrouded in a layer of dust. I wondered if any survivors had been here. It didn't seem like it. Maybe the food would still be there.

"Kitchen?" I asked.

She smiled, not like a lion or a mouse, but like a peaceful creature, content with its knowledge of the world. It made my heart skip a beat – I know, because I was measuring my heart rate at that exact moment. I didn't know whether we would ever talk about what happen on the M6, but I wanted her to know how much I admired her for what she did.

I looked to her. "Lana, thank you."

She held up a hand. "Natali." She laughed, a smile formed so broad, so lovely. "Can I be honest?"

I nodded.

"I didn't think it would go that well. I thought I would distract them as you got away. I was so calm, calmer than I have ever been. I was ready to die, ready to go." She laughed, almost manically. "I've been ready to go for so long now." My chest grew heavy at her words, but her tone was light. "Race you to the kitchen." She winked. It was new, mischievous. I let a crooked smile form on my lips, and we were away.

We had no idea where the kitchen was in this place, but we used our logic. We ran down musty halls that gave birth to rooms. We spotted a study, a library, one of those bullshit masculine smoking rooms with leather chairs and solid crystal ash trays. I lost Lana somewhere in those halls and found her in the huge kitchen below the house. She stood before a pantry, arms wide, hands still resting on the doors to it, like a messiah on a cross. She had never looked so homely, so wife-like to me, so comforting and yet so strong.

She turned her head as I approached, teeth bared, brown eyes full of what I can only describe as glee. I rested my head on her shoulder, wrapped my hands around her thin waist. I could almost feel her ribs through her coat, feel her shudder against my touch, not with disgust, but with lust.

We made love for the last time on the floor of that pantry. Laughing, surrounded by months of food – all the things we had missed for so long. It was everything we needed right then, everything apart from Cain.

After, we opened a jar each of whatever we wanted and talked and laughed with our mouths completely full. Lana even flicked some of the canned peach juice at my face, giggling. She kissed it from my cheek and gazed at me like she used to.

"Can Fort William wait?" I asked, my fingertips running the length of her face.

"It can now." She raised a can to me and laughed at her own joke.

"The world doesn't seem so heavy in this pantry." My arm rested on a sack of potatoes that had sprouted, long pale stems supported faded leaves.

Lana looked around and let her head drop to lean against the wooden walls. "I wonder what Cain would have picked to eat first."

"Peaches – like you. He would have picked the peaches," I said, not breaking my gaze with her.

Her smile faded. She stood slowly, grimaced like she was aching. "I'm going to run. I'll find us the biggest bedroom, the one the bastard Lord of this place would shag his mistresses in." She yawned, stretched her arms.

I laughed, but a crease emerged on my brow as she jogged away. I couldn't work out if her depression was fading, or if she had become manic. It felt like she was hiding something, like when we got the call we had been approved for Cain's adoption. That day she answered the phone, kept it to herself even though the information was slipping out in smiles and sparkling looks of adornment towards me. She told me over dinner that night. The words burst from her as soon as the meal touched the tablecloth. We had never been so happy.

I stood, thought about a logical way to make sure the food was utilised correctly, and began ordering it. Firstly, by portability. I took things that were light, like pasta and noodles, and loaded tote bags I found. We would take this with us when we started to head north again. Then, I looked at the cans and their best-before dates and rearranged them so we ate the older cans before the newer ones. We could live in this place for months. I lined seasonings up next, for no particular reason other than to show-off to Lana that we finally had salt.

I heard a shuffling above my head. Lana sounded like she was jogging down the halls above. I took two cans of vegetable stew and went to find her.

I ran too, realised I hadn't met my goal line – or maybe I had. I didn't check my heart rate when we were making love. I didn't want to risk anything. I ran up and down the carpeted stairs a few times, cans tucked under my arm, until I peaked. Then I went to find my wife.

She was laying on the four-poster bed in a grand room. She had a blanket wrapped around her, a cigarette in one hand.

"Where did you find them?"

"On the nightstand. Dirty bastard." She exhaled smoke into the dim light.

71

I switched on the torch in my pocket and placed the cans on said nightstand. She passed me a cigarette. At first, I refused, but the look in her eye made me think of a simpler time, a time where we just worried about the odd homophobic slur on the streets of London, not a plague that had wiped out most of the country.

I took one, let Lana light it for me.

"You remember when Cain cut a hole in that kid's backpack when he bullied him for having two mums?" she asked.

I smiled. "I told you he'd fight the patriarchy too."

"Like us," she said, her eyes toppling to my face. "We won."

That night, each time I ran, I worried. Something was broken in her. I couldn't understand why I had been given my old Lana back, the woman, the warrior. Her bravery had taken my breath away. Was I dreaming? Was I somewhere else – heaven? It didn't make sense. My teeth still chattered from the cold, my heart still raced when I ran, my stomach still panged for food. But she was different, or the same, the same as when we first met.

Just before dawn, I woke again.

Lana wasn't beside me.

I jogged to the staircase I had been using to raise my heart rate. She was outside, on the large porch inviting you into the mansion. The sun was rising, she was watching Tiger-Lilly graze, and in her hand was a hot drink, steam rising from it into the crisp air. It was a dream – it had to be.

She had coffee, was wrapped in a dressing gown watching the sun rise. It felt like our honeymoon, when each morning that week, she rose early to catch the sun. She said she wanted to make the most of a foreign sunrise. We honeymooned in Brighton – we couldn't afford much, but she made every moment as special as if we went off to a warm tropical land.

She heard me approach. "Natali, I love you."

I took one of her hands from her coffee and placed it between mine. "Lana, talk to me. What's wrong?"

"Can't a woman be happy we found shelter?"

"Yes, but I need to know what you're thinking." I touched her forehead.

"Don't get suspicious that I'm content, Natali. It'll make it go away."

She was right. I didn't want to scare away her happiness – it was too special.

"I feel tired. I'm going to get a few more hours." Her eyes dropped.

"When did you last run?"

"Thirty minutes ago."

"Okay. I'll wake you for the next one. I love you, Lana. I know you know that, but I want you to feel that too."

She kissed me. Delicate at first, but there was a sense of wanting on her lips. She pushed her coffee into my chest as we parted.

"Finish it," she said.

She refused to get out of that bed, even when I told her how many women had probably been fucked by some rich white man in it. I pulled the covers from her, let her bare skin be touched by the cold stagnant air. I'm sure my cries could be heard from outside, but they were more than cries, they were grief itself, rising from my soul and infecting the air around us.

"Lana, baby, please," I begged. "You can't do this to me. You have to fight."

"It's too late now. I made my mind up. I've fought hard enough. I fought against myself, my desires, my attractions, then

73

I fought a fucking homophobic world, fought the law to get our child, fought to make sure he lived, but Tali, Natali, my love." She grew quiet and let out a breathless laugh. "I'm fighting myself again and I can't win this one. I can't keep going anymore. How come everyone else gets to die but me? Please let me be with Cain."

She wept. Each tear that streamed down my face, she caught. Each tear that fell down hers, she let drop to her chest.

"You're an atheist," I said, sobbing, whimpering.

"I know. But the nothingness will make the grief go. You have to understand that, Tali. I decided yesterday I was done, and if I was done, I would die to give you a chance. But I didn't die. I killed those men like Wonder Woman herself forced my hand, but the feeling didn't go away."

"What feeling?"

"The longing to just rest, to have blackness, nothing, instead of grief and fear."

"What about me, Lana? You're leaving me."

"I'm not your Lana anymore. You've known that for some time. This new world changed everything."

"But you are, you were, last night, this morning."

"Because I felt relief. Because I finally decided to let the Sloth take me, Tali."

"It's selfish," I spat. "You're being so selfish." Tears stained my face, my neck. They had even worked their way down to my chest, where they settled between my breasts like they were hiding from her.

"Being selfish is staying alive, staying miserable, pulling you down whilst you're still trying to fight. You still shine so bright, Tali. You have so much fight left in you. I have nothing, not anymore, not since we killed Cain. There is nothing inside my chest

– let me at least have peace with the nothing."

"I thought you were getting better? The horses, they made you smile."

"They died, Tali. They died, like everything does when it's done, and I'm done now." The lioness closed its jaws. The mouse curled up in a tight ball.

I stayed by her side until her heart stopped. I touched her skin, stroked her hair. Each hour that passed slowed her heart. I only left her to run, every three hours. Even though I didn't want to, even though I wanted to die with her in that sordid bed. Someone once told me not to marry the person you can live with, but to marry the person you can't live without. I couldn't live without Lana. But she said I wouldn't have to, that the memories we had together would be the life we shared. That would never be undone.

When she couldn't lift her arms to catch the tears falling from my face, she spoke her last words. "Don't do what we did to Cain. It's not your responsibility this time; it's mine, and mine alone. I made this choice." She whimpered like the words were caught inside her throat, scratching at her soft flesh to be free.

When she couldn't speak anymore, I sang to her, out of tune, sobs echoing through the lyrics. You and me, Babe, how 'bout it? I talked to her about moments in our life, about Cain. I didn't leave out the sad parts, I felt like they were as important as the happy parts.

When she couldn't blink anymore, I closed her eyes for her and caressed her face. I told her how beautiful she was. I told her that she was my goddess, my Gaia, my everything. I told her I would fight like she had on the M6, that I would stay at the mansion until the food had gone, then I would get back on the road and travel to Fort William during the spring, and it would be easy, it would be nice, and I wouldn't be alone because Tiger-Lilly would be there. I told her I loved her the first time I saw her. I told her I was hers.

When she couldn't breathe anymore, I laid my head on her chest until her heart finally stopped. I didn't run for hours; I didn't need to. My heart rate stayed above the goal line like my body was allowing me space to grieve. My love, my Lana. I'll keep running for you. Happy ten-year Anniversary.

FORT WILLIAM

I rode Tiger-Lilly to Fort William. Once alone, she came to me for comfort, for a reminder of the bond she had shared with her herd. She looked at me differently after Lana died, and I looked at her differently too. We both lost something more than a loved one. We lost something flawed, lost the cracks across our hearts that came from our family. There would be new cracks, I was sure, but the cracks Lana caused in my heart were the sweetest damage I could have ever wanted, buried and burning deep inside my chest.

After some time, I was thankful she had the nothingness she needed. I had once craved the nothingness, back when Cain had first died. I wanted nothingness in the place of the crunch the knife made as I put him out of his misery. I wanted nothingness to blanket over the cruelty of missing Lana's smile. I wanted the nothingness to drown out the feelings of rejection that had swallowed me whole.

But Lana's darkness gave me hope, gave me something to fight for. She gave me the lightness back, and for that, I would accept her decision to die, her choice to have peace, and the nothingness.

It took me until late Spring to make it to my destination. Round the coast, avoiding the roads, making sure Tiger-Lilly had enough to graze on. I started keeping a closer eye on her, but she never got Sloth. Neither did I, despite me wanting it so badly, sometimes.

Lana had left an impression on the collapsed UK. When I entered the visitor centre at Ben Nevis, I was greeted by Mohamed. He threw his arms around me and asked for Lana. I shook my head. He held me closer, his body noticeably more filled out, his beard a few inches longer, settling on my shoulder. They were both clean, cleaner than any humans I had seen in some time. My heart panged at the familiar welcome, like Lana had organised them to be there for me. A relieved tear tried to edge its way from my eye. I held it back, told it that I was done with tears.

"The Safaris went south again," Mo told me.

Ryan signed, "People started fighting back."

"Lana fought back," I said, signing and speaking. "Killed a few of them. Right before she died."

"It only needs to start with one," Mo said. There was a glint in his eye. Hope, maybe? Or was it something else? Either way, he seemed like a statesman, not the kind born into politics, but the kind impassioned into it. He straightened his dark coat with its seams that were neat and unfrayed. "We made contact with a lab down in London. They're working on a therapy."

"I know. That's what the Safari was doing, Mo. Bringing fresh corpses to a lab."

His smile faded. "I know, Tali. The team down there didn't know where the bodies were coming from. They've got their own problems to deal with now."

He introduced me to a young woman, ginger hair, freckles over her face like paint splashes. She was pregnant; it was his child. Ryan told me they had lost Daniel a month ago in Milton Keynes. Sloth didn't get him. The Safari didn't get him. He died of flu. He had asthma, couldn't get the treatment. It scared Mohamed into coming north to Fort William, so he could keep his child and new girlfriend safe.

"When civilisation collapses, I guess you either gotta stay rogue or start it again. I wanted to start something again, something new for my kid, so they don't ever see a glass ceiling or a class-based society. So, we came here to put our all in." He passed me a clipboard. "Put your details down here. Write what you used to do before. We'll match you up with a job that suits."

"I worked as a barista and took care of our kid."

He pointed a finger at the sheet. "Write teacher then, if you want to. We all have a chance to reinvent ourselves now."

I stared at the sheet for some time before I wrote EQUINE TRAINER after catching a glimpse of Tiger-Lilly outside. The horses had been helpful to us, they would be helpful to others. I could even ask Mohamed to look at their stats, see if they had their own goal line for Sloth.

I looked to Mohamed's girlfriend. Her stomach sported a small bump already. "What are you going to do when Mandy gets too big to run?" I asked him once she was out of earshot.

"I got the drugs. Only a few months' worth, but its backup for those who can't run. Found them in a Safari truck abandoned on the M6. Few dead guys around, shot."

I smiled, handed him back the clipboard. He added it to a pile on the visitor centre's counter. There were three CrossFit machines lined up behind it.

"Here," I said, handing him the Freddo I kept in my bag's pocket. "Give it to Mandy. Lana was going to eat it for Cain's birthday. She didn't make it that far, but maybe you two can split it on your child's birthday."

He held onto my hand in response. "I am sorry. I am so sorry about your wife, mate."

"She knew what she was doing, what she was teaching me. I can't say I'll have a better life without her, but maybe more people will, because of her."

"You two were a good match. It was an honour to have met her."

"How many more people?" I asked, avoiding words that made my tears come.

He handed me the manifest. "Thirty-three now, and a half." He looked to Mandy. "Mostly Scots. Few of them are part of the mountain rescue up here, know how to live with the land, the hills. We're just heading up to the work site. The huts will be ready soon. Good time of year to start up there."

Mohamed led me up the mountain trail, not all the way, but high enough. A sign greeted us, Base Camp. Nestled into the peaty hills were pods, huts of sorts, like the kind hipsters pay a lot to rent for a weekend away from London. Some were half built, some already had people in them. Fires burned in the open, children ran from hut to hut playing hide and seek with each other, their Scottish accents a delight to my ears. A clock loomed large above, supported by a tripod of branches, each multiple of three on the clockface was highlighted in red. A man was digging the foundations of another hut, wiping beads of sweat from his forehead and coating it with mud by mistake. I smiled, the kind of smile that would have slipped out of Lana without her knowing.

Joanne Askew is a Science-Fiction and Horror writer. She explores mental health issues, sexual identity, femininity and neurodiversity through speculative fiction. As an LGBTQIA+ activist, she believes that fiction will make our world a better place to come out in. She strives for more queer representation in media, particularly speculative fiction, and highlights social injustices like inner-city poverty, the justice system and mental health representation. Joanne has OCD but battles her compulsions to make sure she uses them as a superpower in an empowering way.

www.jaskewauthor.com

Lightning Source UK Ltd.
Milton Keynes UK
UKHW042144161221
395703UK00002B/194

9 781608 641802